GEPT

新制 全民英檢

初級初試模擬試題

10回 滿分

| 試題＋詳解 |

EZ TALK 編輯部著　Judd Piggott 審訂

前言

全民英檢（GEPT）自 2021 年起調整初、中、中高級題型，配合 108 新課綱，這次改制更著重素養題。

初級測驗部分，聽力測驗的題型與題數不變，閱讀測驗第一部分原本考「詞彙和結構」，改為只考「詞彙」。第二部分「段落填空」新增了文意理解題，也就是增加選項為句子或子句的題型。考生需理解上下文含意，理清因果邏輯，才能正確答題。第三部分「閱讀理解」，原本每個題組只有一篇文章，現在部分題組變成多文本題，也就是有一篇以上的文章，考生須具備資訊整合的能力，因為題目的答案可能須根據兩種文本才能正確作答。

為因應此次改版，EZ TALK 打造了補教名師團隊，負責撰寫考題、解說與翻譯，最終完成了這本最完善的《GEPT 新制全民英檢初級初試模擬試題 10 回滿分 試題 + 詳解》，詳盡的解說對於自學，或是老師與家長教學都十分方便。本書文章與試題難易度比英檢初級程度略難，部分文章有少量單字超出英檢初級範圍，但就算不懂也不影響作答。習慣偏難的題目後，真正上考場也能輕鬆解題。最後音檔的設計方便聆聽，可以單獨點選單個回合或是每個問題，不管是做測驗或是檢討錯題皆很方便，學習最有效率。

祝福考生皆能善用此書，並在全民英檢初級初試拿高分，順利通過初試！

目次

初級全民英檢測驗新制說明

	測驗項目	題型	題數	測驗時間
初試	聽力測驗	第一部分：看圖辨義	5 題	約 20 分鐘
		第二部分：問答	10 題	
		第三部分：簡短對話	10 題	30 題
		第四部分：短文聽解	5 題	
	閱讀測驗	第一部分：詞彙	10 題	35 分鐘
		第二部分：段落填空	8 題	30 題
		第三部分：閱讀理解	12 題	

成績計算方式

◆ 聽力測驗與閱讀測驗滿分皆為 120 分。

◆ 聽力測驗與閱讀測驗成績總和達 160 分，且其中任一項成績不低於 72 分，
即通過初試。

測驗分數換算表

答對題數	分數
30	120
29	116
28	112
27	108
26	104
25	100
24	96
23	92
22	88
21	84
20	80
19	76
18	72
17	68
16	64

答對題數	分數
15	60
14	56
13	52
12	48
11	44
10	40
9	36
8	32
7	28
6	24
5	20
4	16
3	12
2	8
1	4

把聽力測驗和閱讀測驗答對題數對應的分數相加，即為成績總和。

舉例說明：小明聽力測驗答對 22 題，閱讀測驗答對 25 題，對應的分數為 88 分和 100 分，兩項成績皆高於 72 分，表示通過初試，且總和為 188 分。

音檔使用說明

STEP ❶

立即註冊

👤 帳號　限3-21碼小寫英文數字

✉ 信箱

🔒 密碼　限8-24碼小寫英文數字

　　再次輸入密碼

完成

或

社群帳號註冊

f 使用Facebook註冊

Google 使用Goole註冊

掃描書中 QRCode

STEP ❷

👤 帳號　請輸入電子郵件

🔒 密碼　請輸入密碼

登入

快速註冊 | 忘記密碼

或

f 使用Facebook登入

Google 使用Goole登入

快速註冊或登入 EZCourse

STEP ❸

請回答以下問題完成訂閱

一、請問本書第65頁，紅色框線中的英文＿＿＿＿是什麼？

二、請問本書第33頁，紅色框線中的英文＿＿＿＿是什麼？

答案　請注意大小寫

答案　請注意大小寫

送出

回答問題按送出

答案就在書中（需注意空格與大小寫）。

STEP ❹

TOEFL iBT 新制托福聽力高分指南

完成訂閱

該書右側會顯示「**已訂閱**」，
表示已成功訂閱，
即可點選播放本書音檔。

STEP ❺

點選個人檔案

查看「**我的訂閱紀錄**」
會顯示已訂閱本書，
點選封面可到本書線上聆聽。

GEPT
初級模擬試題
第1回

聽力測驗

本測驗分四個部分，全部都是單選題，共30題，作答時間約20分鐘。作答說明為中文，印在試題冊上並經由放音機播出。

第一部分　看圖辨義　◀)) 01-001～01-006

共5題，每題請聽放音機播出題目和三個英語句子後，選出與所看到的圖畫最相符的答案。每題只播出一遍。

示範例題

你會看到

你會聽到

Look at the picture. What is the man's job?
(A) He is a painter.
(B) He is a reporter.
(C) He is a salesman

正確答案為 (C)。

聽力測驗

聽力測驗第一部分試題從本頁開始。

Question 1

Question 2

Question 3

開始時間	
結束時間	

Question 4

Question 5

共10題，每題請聽放音機播出題目和三個英語句子後，再從試題冊上三個回答中，選出一個最適合的答案。每題只播出一遍。

示範例題

你會聽到

Does anyone know how the machine works?

你會看到

(A) Why don't you read this note?
(B) I don't know how to cook it, either.
(C) No one has to work late today.

正確答案為 (A)。

6. (A) I've been doing this for days.
   (B) Yeah, I'll be leaving tomorrow.
   (C) Sorry, I've been really busy lately.

7. (A) I'm fine, thank you.
   (B) Better late than never.
   (C) It's great. What's it called?

8. (A) Yes, she has curly hair.
   (B) He's my friend from L.A.
   (C) Oh, that's Ray's cousin, Tina.

9. (A) Yes, I work at a coffee shop.
   (B) Sure, a coffee sounds great.
   (C) Can you pass the cream, please?

10. (A) My friends will arrive soon.
    (B) I'm too busy to answer the phone now.
    (C) Can you ask them to wait in the living room?

11. (A) Sure, I'd love to.
    (B) I believe they're mine, too.
    (C) No, it's not. I think it belongs to May.

12. (A) It's been raining all week.
    (B) I don't know. I'll check later.
    (C) It was nice and dry. We enjoyed it.

13. (A) I have no idea what this is all about.
    (B) Yes. I'll call you when I get home.
    (C) No. We can talk about it tonight.

14. (A) Yes, I'm going there next Monday.
    (B) I've known Mr. Lee for years.
    (C) Yes, I did. He took me to a fancy restaurant.

15. (A) Sorry, I don't have a pen.
    (B) No, but I'd like to get one.
    (C) My favorite animal is the rabbit.

第三部分　簡短對話　🔊 01-018～01-028

共10題，每題請聽放音機播出一段對話和一個相關的問題後，再從試題冊上三個選項中，選出一個最適合的答案。每段對話和問題播出一遍。

示範例題

你會聽到

（男）I can't go any faster.

（女）But the next one is at 1:40. We will be late for the test for sure.

（男）Which platform should we go to?

（女）Platform 2. It's just right near the entrance.

（男）I think we can make it in time.

Question: Where are the man and the woman?

你會看到

(A) At the airport.

(B) At the train station.

(C) In the swimming pool.

正確答案為 (B)。

16. (A) He's injured.
    (B) He's old.
    (C) He's sick.

17. (A) Go to a bakery.
    (B) Bake an apple pie.
    (C) Open a shop on the corner.

18. (A) On the desk.
    (B) We don't know.
    (C) In the woman's purse.

19. (A) He can't do what the woman asked him to do.
    (B) He will buy some food at the supermarket.
    (C) He feels bad that he wasn't invited to the picnic.

20. (A) She missed her train.
    (B) She missed her meeting.
    (C) She didn't hear her alarm clock.

21. (A) A bowl.
    (B) A counter.
    (C) A kind of food.

22. (A) Someone will visit them.
    (B) They will buy sunglasses.
    (C) The man will help the woman.

23. (A) In a taxi.
    (B) At a restaurant.
    (C) At a supermarket.

24. (A) He has to take care of his kid.
    (B) He's busy preparing for a presentation.
    (C) He's sick and has to stay home and rest.

25. (A) By taxi.
    (B) By bus.
    (C) By car.

第四部分　短文聽解　　◀》01-029～01-034

共5題，每題有三個圖片選項。請聽放音機播出的題目，並選一個最適合的圖片。每題播出一遍。

示範例題

你會看到

(A)

Mon	Tue	Wed	Thur.	Fri.	Sat.	Sun.
⛈	🌧	🌧	⛅	⛅	☀	☀

(B)

Mon	Tue	Wed	Thur.	Fri.	Sat.	Sun.
⛈	🌧	🌧	⛅	⛅	⛅	⛅

(C)

Mon	Tue	Wed	Thur.	Fri.	Sat.	Sun.
⛈	🌧	☀	☀	☀	☀	☀

你會聽到

Listen to the weather forecast. What's the weather like next week?

This is Good Day weather forecast. It's been hot these days. Are you worried whether it is going to be this hot next week? Then, there is good news for you. We are going to have rain for three days next week which is going to bring down the temperature a little bit. Thursday and Friday are cloudy. And we can expect clear days on the weekends.

正確答案為 (A)。

(A)

(B)
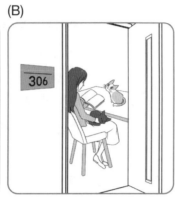

(C)

Question 27

(A)

(B)

(C)

Question 28

(A)

(B)

(C)

Question 29

(A)

(B)

(C)

Question 30

(A)

✈ DEPARTURES				
TIME	DESTINATION	FLIGHT	GATE	REMARKS
08:00	NEW YORK	BR 23z9	20	IN FLIGHT
08:20	TOKYO	AC 336	24	BOARDING
08:30	PARIS	FR 208	35	ON TIME
09:00	ROME	AZ 873	40	ON TIME

(B)

TRAIN INFORMATION					
TIME	NUMBER	TRAIN	TO	FROM	PLATFORM
08:00	32	EXPRESS	ROME	VENICE	2
09:00	42	LOCAL	FLORENCE	VENICE	3
09:10	20	ICE	VENICE	NICE	1
09:30	10	EXPRESS	NAPOLI	ROME	4

(C)

FREE SHUTTLE BUS SERVICE

NEW YORK TO BROOKLYN	BROOKLYN TO NEW YORK
8:00 AM	7:50 AM
8:20 AM	8:10 AM
8:40 AM	8:30 AM
9:00 AM	8:50 AM

閱讀測驗

本測驗分三部分，全部都是單選題，共30題，作答時間35分鐘。

第一部分　詞彙

共10題，每個題目裡有一個空格。請從四個選項中選出一個最適合題意的字或詞作答。

1. There's been an accident. Can someone please call _____ ?
   (A) a clerk
   (B) a medicine
   (C) an ambulance
   (D) a businessman

2. Do you know how we can _____ the waterfall?
   (A) arrive to
   (B) get to
   (C) reach to
   (D) go on

3. Preparing for tests and doing my homework _____ a lot of time.
   (A) cost
   (B) take
   (C) spend
   (D) pay

4. To take a photo, simply push this _____ .
   (A) cotton
   (B) curtain
   (C) button
   (D) bottom

5. Mike is a good worker, so I don't think he missed the meeting _____ .
   (A) on purpose
   (B) by accident
   (C) on time
   (D) by mistake

6. I haven't _____ Tina in three years.
   (A) heard of
   (B) heard about
   (C) heard from
   (D) heard out

7. Robert Johnson is the only _____ I like in that movie.
   (A) player
   (B) actor
   (C) dentist
   (D) audience

8. What's a good store to buy _____ for my art class?
   (A) supplies
   (B) clothes
   (C) snacks
   (D) paintings

9. When you have too many choices, it can be hard to _____ .
   (A) express yourself
   (B) take your time
   (C) forgive others
   (D) make a decision

10. Learning new things is fun! _____ , it can be difficult sometimes.
    (A) In the end
    (B) By the way
    (C) On the one hand
    (D) On the other hand

共8題，包括二個段落，每個段落含四個空格。每格均有四個選項，請依照文意選出最適合的答案。

Questions 11-14

This morning, our neighbor, Ms. Green, saw Toby almost get _____(11)_____ by a taxi when he was crossing the street. Toby was checking his phone and not paying attention to traffic. "Watch out!" Ms. Green shouted when she saw the taxi _____(12)_____ toward him. _____(13)_____ Fortunately, he only broke his phone. The situation _____(14)_____ have been a lot worse. After being lectured by his parents and his teacher, Toby decided that he would never look at his phone while crossing the street again.

11. (A) run around   (B) run after   (C) run over   (D) run thorough

12. (A) reaching   (B) rolling   (C) coming   (D) leaving

13. (A) Toby put his phone in his pocket.
    (B) Toby stopped and dropped his phone.
    (C) Toby walked and held his phone.
    (D) Toby smiled and waved to Ms. Green.

14. (A) will   (B) should   (C) can   (D) could

Questions 15-18

I have always loved the story of how my parents met. My dad was born and raised in London and has a great ___(15)___ in Turner's paintings. That's why 20 years ago, when a friend of his told him that there was a Turner exhibit in Berlin, he decided to go. ___(16)___ was that it is also the place where he would meet my mom. It happened after my dad saw the exhibit and ___(17)___ to go back to the hotel and have dinner. My mom was standing at the exit of the gallery, holding a map and looking lost. He walked up to her and ___(18)___ help. And the rest is history.

15. (A) fear   (B) information   (C) interest   (D) knowledge

16. (A) When he didn't go
     (B) Why he didn't know
     (C) What he didn't know
     (D) Where he didn't go

17. (A) pay attention   (B) was about   (C) fell behind   (D) found out

18. (A) asked for   (B) sent for   (C) went to   (D) offered to

共12題，包括4個題組，每個題組含1至2篇短文，與數個相關的四選一的選擇題。請由試題上的選項中選出最適合的答案。

Questions 19-21

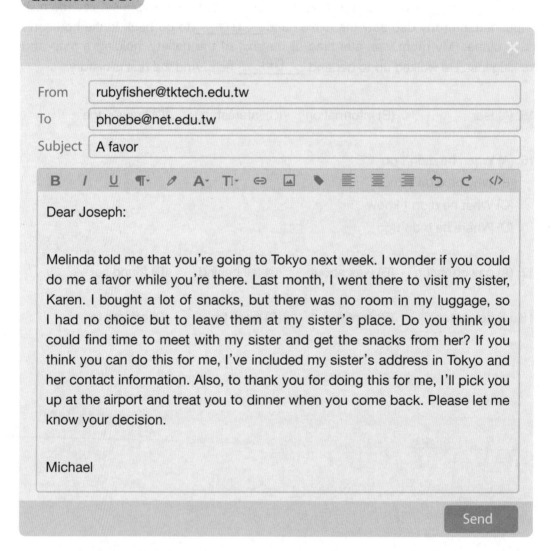

From rubyfisher@tktech.edu.tw

To phoebe@net.edu.tw

Subject A favor

B I U ¶▾ ✎ A▾ T▾ ⇔ 🖻 🏷 ≣ ≣ ≣ ↺ ↻ </>

Dear Joseph:

Melinda told me that you're going to Tokyo next week. I wonder if you could do me a favor while you're there. Last month, I went there to visit my sister, Karen. I bought a lot of snacks, but there was no room in my luggage, so I had no choice but to leave them at my sister's place. Do you think you could find time to meet with my sister and get the snacks from her? If you think you can do this for me, I've included my sister's address in Tokyo and her contact information. Also, to thank you for doing this for me, I'll pick you up at the airport and treat you to dinner when you come back. Please let me know your decision.

Michael

Send

Karen Wu

Phone number: +81(0)3-5228-8107

Address: 1-3 Kagurazaka,

Shinjuku-ku, Tokyo 162-8601, Japan

P.S. She can only be reached in the daytime before five o'clock.

19. What can we learn about Michael?

(A) He left something in Japan.

(B) His sister is always available.

(C) He didn't bring luggage on his trip.

(D) He wants to send something to his sister.

20. What is the main reason that Michael wrote this e-mail?

(A) To ask Joseph to help him.

(B) To thank Joseph for helping him.

(C) To find time to meet with Karen.

(D) To apologize for not being careful.

21. Which of the following is true?

(A) Karen's e-mail is written on the note.

(B) Karen lives in Tokyo, Japan at present.

(D) Joseph has agreed to do Michael a favor.

(C) Michael offered to give Joseph some snacks.

The Komodo dragon, also known as the Komodo monitor, is a species of lizard that can only be found in Indonesia. It is the largest lizard in the world, with some individuals reaching lengths of up to 10 feet and weighing over 150 pounds. They have strong jaws and sharp teeth, making them powerful **predators**. Their diet includes birds, snakes and even deer. Komodo Dragons are also skilled climbers and swimmers, and they can move quickly when they hunt for food.

Unfortunately, the number of Komodo Dragons is getting smaller because they are losing their homes and people are hunting them. To keep them safe, they are now a protected species. People are working hard to take care of them and make sure they survive. Indonesia even created the Komodo National Park to protect these amazing animals.

In short, the Komodo Dragon is a large lizard found only in Indonesia. They are both large and unique. It's important to protect them and their homes and tell others about why it's necessary to take care of them. This way, we can make sure they keep existing for a long time.

22. Which is true about Komodo Dragons?
    (A) They don't exist anymore.
    (B) Their size is still increasing.
    (C) They eat fruit and vegetables.
    (D) They aren't allowed to be hunted.

23. What does the word "predator" mean?
    (A) An animal that eats other animals.
    (B) An animal that protects other animals
    (C) A friendly animal that kids can play with.
    (D) An animal that is eaten by other animals.

24. Where would we likely find this article?
    (A) In a modern history book
    (B) On a national park website
    (C) In a magazine for pet owners
    (D) At the entrance to an aquarium

Dear Gina,

How have you been lately? I came to visit my grandparents a few weeks ago and I've been staying with them since then.

My grandparents own a <u>hostel</u> in downtown Seoul. They're busy hosting travelers from all over the world every day. In the morning, I help my grandfather clean the rooms and common areas, and my grandma prepares breakfast for all the guests. In the afternoon, my grandfather takes travelers hiking in the mountains while my grandmother shows others around downtown Seoul.

All the guests here have a pleasant stay, and some of them even said they will definitely choose to stay at our hostel next time they visit Korea. This had been such a fantastic experience, and I hope you can come with me when I visit next year. You can even stay at the hostel for free!

Love,
Mindy

25. What is a "hostel"?

    (A) a restaurant

    (B) a school

    (C) a store

    (D) a hotel

26. What is Mindy doing in Korea?

    (A) She opened a hostel with her grandparents in Seoul.

    (B) She takes travelers to experience the beauty of Seoul.

    (C) She is helping her grandparents with their business.

    (D) She is inviting people from all over the world to visit.

27. Which is true about the story?

    (A) Mindy helps keep the hostel tidy.

    (B) Mindy is not in South Korea now.

    (C) Mindy's grandmother enjoys hiking.

    (D) Gina is going to visit Korea next year.

Questions 28-30

Since my father had to go on a business trip to France, our family stayed in Paris for a week. While my dad was working during the day, my mother and I visited all the famous spots in Paris. We went to the Eiffel Tower, the famous Louvre Museum, and had a picnic at a beautiful park. It was so much fun. Although we don't speak French, the locals were so kind and offered help when we needed it. We also went to Galeries Lafayette Haussmann, where my mom bought a purse and some new clothes for me and my dad. After that, we met my dad at a French restaurant and had a nice dinner.

I spent the rest of my free time with my uncle Daniel, who moved to France two years ago. He took me to places that are rarely visited by tourists. He even took me to a restaurant where I tried escargots—snails—for the very first time! I had a great time with my uncle. I'll definitely come visit him again.

28. What type of place is the Galeries Lafayette Haussmann?
    (A) A museum
    (B) A restaurant
    (C) A supermarket
    (D) A department store

29. Which of the following is true?
    (A) The writer's father went to Paris for work.
    (B) The writer's mother is able to speak French.
    (C) The writer met Daniel for the first time in Paris.
    (D) Daniel took the writer's parents to a restaurant.

30. What is true about the trip?
    (A) Daniel took the writer shopping.
    (B) The people there all speak English.
    (C) The writer tried a new kind of food.
    (D) A guide took them to tourist spots in Paris.

GEPT
初級模擬試題
第 2 回

02-000

第 2 回聽力測驗

聽力測驗

本測驗分四個部分，全部都是單選題，共30題，作答時間約20分鐘。作答說明為中文，印在試題冊上並經由放音機播出。

第一部分 **看圖辨義** ◀)) 02-001～02-006

共5題，每題請聽放音機播出題目和三個英語句子後，選出與所看到的圖畫最相符的答案。每題只播出一遍。

示範例題

你會看到

你會聽到

Look at the picture. What is the man's job?
(A) He is a painter.
(B) He is a reporter.
(C) He is a salesman

正確答案為 (C)。

🔊 聽力測驗

聽力測驗第一部分試題從本頁開始。

Question 1

Question 2

Question 3

開始時間	
結束時間	

Question 4

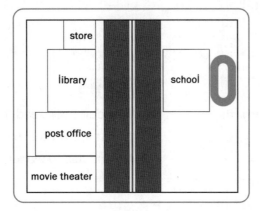

Question 5

共10題，每題請聽放音機播出題目和三個英語句子後，再從試題冊上三個回答中，選出一個最適合的答案。每題只播出一遍。

示範例題

你會聽到

Does anyone know how the machine works?

你會看到

(A) Why don't you read this note?

(B) I don't know how to cook it, either.

(C) No one has to work late today.

正確答案為 (A)。

6. (A) Of course. I don't mind.
   (B) No, I don't. Here!
   (C) Sorry, it's my pen.

7. (A) Actually, I am new here. I'm Jason.
   (B) You're right. This is my home.
   (C) I forget, too. But it's a nice neighborhood.

8. (A) I think I'll wait until they leave.
   (B) I am not sure if I have enough time to practice.
   (C) The school team has won a lot of games.

9. (A) I'd love to. It sounds amazing.
   (B) I can't afford a house right now.
   (C) I don't think anything is wrong with it.

10. (A) Yes, it's a wonderful drawing.
    (B) Pants like that must be expensive.
    (C) I hear it was done by a famous artist.

11. (A) Where to?
    (B) I'd love to.
    (C) Was it fun?

12. (A) Yes, can you help me?
    (B) Black coffee would be great.
    (C) I appreciate it.

13. (A) You mean the one on the coast?
    (B) How long will you stay at the hotel?
    (C) Having a vacation with you is a fun experience.

14. (A) I wonder when it's going to stop.
    (B) Really? Let's check the weather report.
    (C) Time to wash my clothes.

15. (A) In twenty minutes.
    (B) Every thirty minutes.
    (C) Tomorrow.

第三部分　簡短對話　🔊 02-018～02-028

共10題,每題請聽放音機播出一段對話和一個相關的問題後,再從試題冊上三個選項中,選出一個最適合的答案。每段對話和問題播出一遍。

示範例題

你會聽到

（男）I can't go any faster.

（女）But the next one is at 1:40. We will be late for the test for sure.

（男）Which platform should we go to?

（女）Platform 2. It's just right near the entrance.

（男）I think we can make it in time.

Question: Where are the man and the woman?

你會看到

(A) At the airport.

(B) At the train station.

(C) In the swimming pool.

___

正確答案為 (B)。

16. (A) The woman is prettier now.
    (B) The woman is quite old.
    (C) The woman is not as pretty as before.

17. (A) They were chased by a dog.
    (B) The woman ran after the dog.
    (C) Their car hit a dog.

18. (A) At a tea shop.
    (B) At a restaurant.
    (C) At a friend's place.

19. (A) Stay at the office later than usual.
    (B) Cook dinner for himself.
    (C) Get some milk for his wife.

20. (A) The girl is going to the hospital.
    (B) The mother is going to call her husband.
    (C) The girl doesn't feel like seeing a doctor now.

21. (A) He's Anna's friend.
    (B) He works at Anna's office.
    (C) He's a mailman.

22. (A) They are going to rent a car.
    (B) They are going to buy sunglasses and sunscreen.
    (C) They are going to spend time at the beach.

23. (A) The woman forgot her smartphone.
    (B) The woman found a missing watch.
    (C) They bought a gift for Lilian.

24. (A) He's shopping.
    (B) He's ordering.
    (C) He's eating.

25. (A) They're husband and wife.
    (B) They're classmates.
    (C) They're nurses.

第四部分 短文聽解 🔊 02-029～02-034

共5題，每題有三個圖片選項。請聽放音機播出的題目，並選一個最適合的圖片。每題播出一遍。

示範例題

你會看到

(A)

Mon	Tue	Wed	Thur.	Fri.	Sat.	Sun.
🌧️	🌧️	🌧️	🌤️	🌤️	🌥️	☀️

(B)

Mon	Tue	Wed	Thur.	Fri.	Sat.	Sun.
⛈️	🌧️	🌧️	🌤️	🌤️	🌤️	🌤️

(C)

Mon	Tue	Wed	Thur.	Fri.	Sat.	Sun.
⛈️	🌧️	🌤️	☀️	☀️	🌥️	🌥️

你會聽到

Listen to the weather forecast. What's the weather like next week?

This is Good Day weather forecast. It's been hot these days. Are you worried whether it is going to be this hot next week? Then, there is good news for you. We are going to have rain for three days next week which is going to bring down the temperature a little bit. Thursday and Friday are cloudy. And we can expect clear days on the weekends.

正確答案為 (A)。

Question 26

(A)

(B)

(C)

Question 27

(A)

(B)

(C)

Question 28

(A)

(B)

(C)

Question 29

(A)

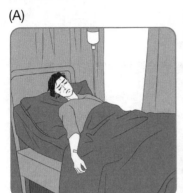

(B)

(C)

Question 30

(A)

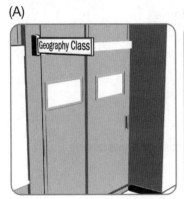

(B)

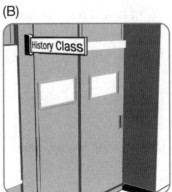

(C)

閱讀測驗

本測驗分三部分，全部都是單選題，共30題，作答時間35分鐘。

第一部分　詞彙

共10題，每個題目裡有一個空格。請從四個選項中選出一個最適合題意的字或詞作答。

1. A: Do you know why Danny is being punished? B: Because he was being _____ to Ms. Chen.
   (A) active
   (B) impolite
   (C) negative
   (D) peaceful

2. Can you pick up a _____ of bread on your way home?
   (A) liter
   (B) loaf
   (C) gram
   (D) foot

3. There's not _____ sugar left since Mandy used most of it yesterday.
   (A) many
   (B) little
   (C) much
   (D) amount

4. I am trying to _____ some weight because my doctor said I'm too thin.
   (A) obtain
   (B) get
   (C) gain
   (D) decrease

5. Rose's husband is taking her to a fancy restaurant, so she's going to wear a _____ dress.
   (A) casual
   (B) colorful
   (C) tight
   (D) formal

6. The soup _____ sour, so I don't really like it.
    (A) sounds
    (B) feels
    (C) tastes
    (D) notices

7. The office is on the twentieth floor! I'm not taking the _____ .
    (A) boat
    (B) stairs
    (C) elevator
    (D) bridge

8. Gina is such a _____ student. She spends a lot of time studying.
    (A) humble
    (B) patient
    (C) humorous
    (D) diligent

9. My sister is interested in cooking and hopes that she can be a _____ one day.
    (A) officer
    (B) chef
    (C) director
    (D) waiter

10. We plan to plant some sunflowers in the _____ .
    (A) stage
    (B) platform
    (C) yard
    (D) library

共8題，包括二個段落，每個段落含四個空格。每格均有四個選項，請依照文意選出最適合
的答案。

Questions 11-14

The boy who moved into our neighborhood last month broke Ms. White's window
with a baseball while he was playing ____(11)____ with a friend. Because he didn't
want to ____(12)____ trouble, he ran away afterwards. However, the boy felt sorry for
____(13)____ , and later admitted that he was the one who broke the window. He also
helped Ms. White fix the broken window, so she ____(14)____ him for his careless
mistake.

11. (A) throw   (B) catch   (C) joke   (D) sport

12. (A) get on   (B) put on   (C) put off   (D) get in

13. (A) how he did it   (B) what to do
    (C) what he had done   (D) who had done it

14. (A) forgave   (B) forgot   (C) blamed   (D) praised

Questions 15-18

A: Lisa still hasn't found her lost rabbit, ____(15)____ ?

B: No, not yet. I hope someone will find it and return it to her soon.

A: I do, too. It was a birthday gift from her dad, so she must be really sad.

B: Oh, Mr. Chen. I ____(16)____ him in ages. He must be busy with work.

A: Actually, Lisa has a younger brother living in Canada, so her dad travels back and forth a lot.

B: So her dad is over there now?

A: Yeah. I think he left for Canada last week. Lisa must be ____(17)____ really upset about her lost rabbit. Maybe we could call her and cheer her up.

B: That's a great idea! I'm sure she'd love to ____(18)____ us.

15. (A) does she   (B) had she   (C) has she   (D) didn't she

16. (A) have seen   (B) saw   (C) haven't seen   (D) didn't see

17. (A) feeling   (B) feel   (C) feels   (D) felt

18. (A) listen to   (B) contact to   (C) hear about   (D) hear from

共12題，包括4個題組，每個題組含1至2篇短文，與數個相關的四選一的選擇題。請由試題上的選項中選出最適合的答案。

Questions 19-21

Read the following department store directory.

FOURTH FLOOR	FURNITURE, BEDDING
THIRD FLOOR	MEN'S CLOTHING
SECOND FLOOR	WOMEN'S CLOTHING
FIRST FLOOR	SHOES, INFORMATION, LOST AND FOUND
BASEMENT	FOOD COURT, GROCERY STORE

19. Where should people go if they lose their wallet?
    (A) The first floor
    (B) The second floor
    (C) The third floor
    (D) The fourth floor

20. Mrs. Wilson wants to buy a coffee table for her living room. Where can she find it?
    (A) The first floor
    (B) The second floor
    (C) The third floor
    (D) The fourth floor

21. The Wilson family wants to have a meal at the department store. Where should they go?
    (A) The basement
    (B) The first floor
    (C) The second floor
    (D) The third floor

Questions 22-24

Wearing a seat belt is one of the best ways to protect yourself on the road. In fact, seat belts can greatly reduce the risk of death in a car crash. That's why it's important for everyone in the car, including the driver and passengers, to buckle up. Failure to do so is also illegal, and can result in a ticket.

However, many people still do not wear their seat belts, especially back seat passengers. We should keep our seat belt on at all times not because we might get a ticket, but because it is the most effective way to stay safe while in a car. The government is working to educate people about the importance of wearing seat belts. They hope that if people better understand the dangers of not buckling up, there will be less injuries and **fatalities**.

22. What does the word "fatalities" likely mean?
    (A) tickets
    (B) deaths
    (C) patients
    (D) accidents

23. What is the best title for this passage?
    (A) *A Ticket to Save Your Life*
    (B) *Buckle Up for Your Safety*
    (C) *How to Avoid Car Accidents*
    (D) *A Message from the Government*

24. According to the passage, which is true?
    (A) Only the driver is required to put on a seatbelt.
    (B) Not wearing a seatbelt while driving is against the law.
    (C) Handing out tickets is the best way to prevent car crashes.
    (D) The government is trying to reduce the number of accidents.

The Grand Tour

You can:

- Stay at luxury hotels
- Enjoy delicious local foods
- Visit famous tourist spots
- Take the fastest train in the world
- Do all the shopping you like at fashionable department stores

Date: July 30 ~ August 5

Price: NT$ 20,000 / adult
　　　NT$ 18,000 / age 12 - 18
　　　NT$ 15,000 / age under 12
　　　(flights, hotels, and train tickets are included)

Call "Get Away" at 1123-6789

Check our website: http://www.getaway.com.tw for more information

** Print out this coupon for **20%** off **

25. The price does not include which of the following?
    (A) hotels
    (B) air travel
    (C) train trips
    (D) souvenirs

26. Mr. and Mrs. Chen have a daughter who is seven years old. They want to join the tour. How much will they have to pay if they use a coupon?
    (A) NT $44,000
    (B) NT $46,400
    (C) NT $55,000
    (D) NT $58,000

27. Which activity on the Grand Tour is a unique experience?
    (A) A train ride
    (B) A hotel stay
    (C) A shopping trip
    (D) A restaurant meal

Jimmy and I were best friends in high school. Both of us wanted to major in English in college and become English teachers. We used to do everything together and had many of the same hobbies and interests. However, something changed after the new transfer student joined our class. Jimmy didn't talk to me as often as he did before, and he spent more time with him than with me. I felt like I was being left out. I wasn't sure what to do, so I went to my teacher, Miss Ou, to talk about my problem. She told me it's very common for friends to become less close, even best friends. She said that I shouldn't take it personally. It was hard to hear that, but I knew that Miss Ou was right. I gave Jimmy some space, focusing on my own life instead. But I still believed one day we would find our way back to each other.

28. Why did the author and Jimmy's friendship change?
    (A) Because they didn't have any common interests.
    (B) Because the author wanted to focus on his own life.
    (C) Because the author transferred to a different school.
    (D) Because Jimmy spent more time with another student.

29. Which of the following is NOT true about Jimmy?
    (A) He is best friends with the author.
    (B) He shares interests with the author.
    (C) He was good friends with the author.
    (D) He goes to the same school as the author.

30. What can we learn from the story?
    (A) Making friends is important.
    (B) Friendship is about forgiving.
    (C) Teachers give the best advice.
    (D) Friendship doesn't always last.

GEPT
初級模擬試題
第3回

03-000

第3回聽力測驗

聽力測驗

本測驗分四個部分，全部都是單選題，共30題，作答時間約20分鐘。作答說明為中文，印在試題冊上並經由放音機播出。

第一部分　看圖辨義　◀》03-001～03-006

共5題，每題請聽放音機播出題目和三個英語句子後，選出與所看到的圖畫最相符的答案。每題只播出一遍。

示範例題

你會看到

你會聽到

Look at the picture. What is the man's job?
(A) He is a painter.
(B) He is a reporter.
(C) He is a salesman

正確答案為 (C)。

聽力測驗

聽力測驗第一部分試題從本頁開始。

Question 1

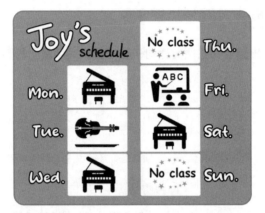

Question 2

Question 3

Question 4

Question 5

共10題，每題請聽放音機播出題目和三個英語句子後，再從試題冊上三個回答中，選出一個最適合的答案。每題只播出一遍。

示範例題

你會聽到

Does anyone know how the machine works?

你會看到

(A) Why don't you read this note?

(B) I don't know how to cook it, either.

(C) No one has to work late today.

正確答案為 (A)。

6. (A) You can get it at the front desk.
   (B) Yes. Here's a towel.
   (C) It's next to the elevator.

7. (A) I don't think it's a good place to go.
   (B) How come?
   (C) This is a great department store.

8. (A) Cindy, right? I met her last summer. She's fun.
   (B) I'm a meat lover, especially beef and chicken.
   (C) You should see a doctor if you hurt your knee.

9. (A) It looks great on you.
   (B) Thank you for the gift.
   (C) The shorts don't fit.

10. (A) At 6:00 PM next Saturday.
    (B) It's going to be at my place.
    (C) Vicky and I are going together.

11. (A) It happens every two weeks.
    (B) We'd better start studying for it.
    (C) What was the test like?

12. (A) I'm going to have a birthday party next week.
    (B) At the park next to the school.
    (C) I painted it in my art class.

13. (A) Why? What have you done?
    (B) When did you go fishing?
    (C) That's so sweet of him.

14. (A) Neither do I. I think we're lost.
    (B) 8:30 will be too late for us.
    (C) But I know who they are.

15. (A) Yes, that movie is great.
    (B) Which movie theater should we go to?
    (C) Yes. That's how I improve my English.

第三部分　簡短對話　◀》03-018～03-028

共10題，每題請聽放音機播出一段對話和一個相關的問題後，再從試題冊上三個選項中，選出一個最適合的答案。每段對話和問題播出一遍。

示範例題

你會聽到

（男）I can't go any faster.

（女）But the next one is at 1:40. We will be late for the test for sure.

（男）Which platform should we go to?

（女）Platform 2. It's just right near the entrance.

（男）I think we can make it in time.

Question: Where are the man and the woman?

你會看到

(A) At the airport.

(B) At the train station.

(C) In the swimming pool.

___

正確答案為 (B)。

16. (A) He thinks the woman's hair is too short.
    (B) He thinks the woman looks better with long hair.
    (C) He thinks the woman looks good with shorter hair.

17. (A) They will probably be caught in the traffic jam.
    (B) They will arrive at the airport in two hours.
    (C) His taxi isn't available today.

18. (A) She can't find Mark.
    (B) She's late to the performance.
    (C) She doesn't know Kevin's number.

19. (A) Wait for his brother.
    (B) Try on the coat.
    (C) Open the box.

20. (A) She changed her mind.
    (B) She would think about the man.
    (C) She didn't want to go after all.

21. (A) To make her dream come true.
    (B) To make a lot of money.
    (C) To sing at a party.

22. (A) He can buy the woman some coffee.
    (B) He doesn't want to pay.
    (C) They can pay without using cash.

23. (A) Don't do it if you don't want to.
    (B) Do it only if you are able to.
    (C) You had better not do it.

24. (A) Yes, she will.
    (B) No, she won't.
    (C) She will, but she'll be late.

25. (A) It has happened before.
    (B) He asked the woman not to do it again.
    (C) He doesn't know what to do.

第四部分 短文聽解 🔊 03-029～03-034

共5題，每題有三個圖片選項。請聽放音機播出的題目，並選一個最適合的圖片。每題播出一遍。

示範例題

你會看到

(A)

Mon	Tue	Wed	Thur.	Fri.	Sat.	Sun.
🌧️	🌧️	🌧️	⛅	⛅	☀️	☀️

(B)

Mon	Tue	Wed	Thur.	Fri.	Sat.	Sun.
⛈️	🌧️	🌧️	⛅	⛅	⛅	⛅

(C)

Mon	Tue	Wed	Thur.	Fri.	Sat.	Sun.
⛈️	🌧️	☀️	☀️	☀️	☀️	☀️

你會聽到

Listen to the weather forecast. What's the weather like next week?

This is Good Day weather forecast. It's been hot these days. Are you worried whether it is going to be this hot next week? Then, there is good news for you. We are going to have rain for three days next week which is going to bring down the temperature a little bit. Thursday and Friday are cloudy. And we can expect clear days on the weekends.

___

正確答案為 (A)。

Question 26

(A)

(B)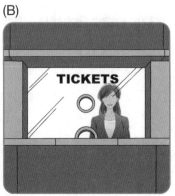

(C)

Question 27

(A)

(B)

(C)

Question 28

(A)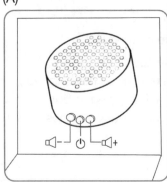

(B)

(C)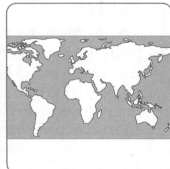

Question 29

(A)
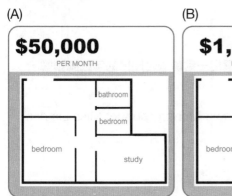

(B)
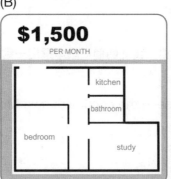

(C)

Question 30

(A)
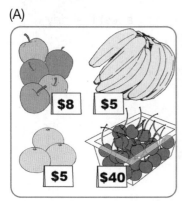

(B)
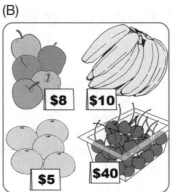

(C)
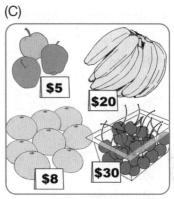

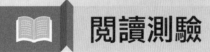

閱讀測驗

本測驗分三部分,全部都是單選題,共30題,作答時間35分鐘。

第一部分 詞彙

共10題,每個題目裡有一個空格。請從四個選項中選出一個最適合題意的字或詞作答。

1. Please _____ me to send the document next Monday so that Miss Lin can receive it on time.
   (A) hope
   (B) allow
   (C) expect
   (D) remind

2. Jacob needs to take Friday off because he has to _____ a test that day.
   (A) post
   (B) take
   (C) delay
   (D) cancel

3. The hotel was _____ , and the room was not even cleaned.
   (A) terrible
   (B) amazing
   (C) ordinary
   (D) marvelous

4. Mr. Lee, a very _____ teacher, doesn't let students in if they're late.
   (A) strict
   (B) patient
   (C) talkative
   (D) effective

5. I'm pretty hungry, so can I have two _____ of pizza?
   (A) bags
   (B) slices
   (C) loaves
   (D) glasses

6. I had a great time on the trip, but I was so _____ after the 12-hour flight back home.
   (A) tired
   (B) excited
   (C) satisfied
   (D) interested

7. After many years of hard work, Jenny finally _____ her goal.
   (A) realized
   (B) imagined
   (C) appreciated
   (D) understood

8. Ray hasn't cleaned his room in months, so it's _____ garbage.
   (A) full of
   (B) made of
   (C) covered with
   (D) crowded with

9. Christopher ate all the cookies; _____ , we had none left for dessert.
   (A) besides
   (B) however
   (C) therefore
   (D) no wonder

10. Bob _____ Mary to do his homework for him.
   (A) said
   (B) asked
   (C) made
   (D) pleased

共8題，包括二個段落，每個段落含四個空格。每格均有四個選項，請依照文意選出最適合的答案。

Questions 11-14

Hey Sylvia,

Just wanted to say thank you for taking me and my family out to dinner while I was in L.A. It was such a pleasant _____(11)_____ to run into you there. We hadn't _____(12)_____ each other since you moved away five years ago. I really enjoyed the food at the restaurant that you _____(13)_____ us to, especially the brownie I had for dessert. I liked it so much that I tried to make some when I _____(14)_____ back home. Now I'm really into baking and I can't wait for you to visit and try my desserts. Anyway, thanks again and keep in touch!

Best,

Emma

11. (A) event　　　(B) matter　　　(C) chance　　　(D) surprise

12. (A) saw　　　(B) see　　　(C) seeing　　　(D) seen

13. (A) visited　　　(B) shared　　　(C) took　　　(D) paid

14. (A) get　　　(B) got　　　(C) will get　　　(D) have got

Questions 15-18

_____(15)_____ you heard of EVs? EV stands for electric vehicle. These are cars that have electric motors rather than gas engines. One of the biggest advantages of EVs _____(16)_____ that they cause no air pollution when running. An EV can even drive _____(17)_____. However, there have been some major accidents caused by EVs. In one case, an EV caught on fire, and the people inside couldn't open the doors. In _____(18)_____, the EV's computer failed, causing the car to crash. People are still worried whether EVs are safe to drive, but one thing we know for sure is that there will be more and more electric cars in the future.

15. (A) Do   (B) Can   (C) Have   (D) Are

16. (A) is   (B) are   (C) will be   (D) have been

17. (A) it   (B) itself   (C) themselves   (D) yourself

18. (A) other   (B) another   (C) the other   (D) one more

共12題，包括4個題組，每個題組含1至2篇短文，與數個相關的四選一的選擇題。請由試題上的選項中選出最適合的答案。

Questions 19-21

Picnic Day!

- 11:00 am, Saturday, June 22, 2024
- Lakeshore Park
- Wear your most comfortable t-shirt and shorts.
- Bring your family and friends along with your favorite snacks
- Enjoy the sandwiches and mini burgers that we've prepared for you!
- The park has tennis and badminton courts, so if you'd like to play, don't forget to bring your own equipment.

Let's have fun together!

Email Ashley three days before the picnic at ashley.davis@citygovernment.com if you plan to come. In case of rain, the picnic will be cancelled, so be sure to watch the weather report the evening before the event.

19. What can people do at Lakeshore Park on June 22?
    (A) Spend time with their friends and family.
    (B) Have fun while wearing their finest clothes.
    (C) Prepare snacks for all the people at the picnic.
    (D) Learn how to make sandwiches and mini burgers.

20. Who was the event likely planned by?

    (A) Lakeshore Park

    (B) The city government

    (C) A food product company

    (D) A maker of sports equipment

21. What is the last possible day to make a decision about going to the picnic?

    (A) June 19

    (B) June 20

    (C) June 21

    (D) June 22

Are you struggling with weight loss? Have you tried different methods but still haven't achieved the body you always wanted? Here is some advice from Dr. Ramies.

1. Eat Right → Eat more meat like chicken, beef and fish.
Have less rice, noodles and bread.
Stay away from snacks.

2. Stay Active → Do exercise that brings your heartbeats up to 130 bpm. (beats per minute)
Exercise for at least 30 minutes, three times a week.

3. Make exercise a habit → Exercising 30 minutes at a time isn't difficult. Most people fail to lose weight not because they can't do it, but because they struggle to continue doing it.

22. Who would be interested in this article?
    (A) Someone who is sick or injured.
    (B) Someone who is experiencing hunger.
    (C) Someone who is dealing with a heart condition.
    (D) Someone who is worried about their body shape.

23. Which of the following is suggested for losing weight?
    (A) Getting 8 hours of sleep.
    (B) Getting regular exercise.
    (C) Not eating meat or bread.
    (D) Taking a weight loss class.

24. How many minutes should people exercise each week?
    (A) At least 30 minutes
    (B) At least 60 minutes
    (C) 90 minutes or more
    (D) Three times a week

Questions 25-27

When visiting or staying with friends in other countries, it's always polite to bring gifts to show your appreciation. But before you give a gift, you should make an effort to learn about the gift giving customs in that country.

Flowers are a common gift, but in many European countries, red roses are a symbol of love, and thus wouldn't be a **suitable** gift for your host. In Japan, your host will appreciate a gift that is carefully wrapped. But don't use white paper, because white is the color of death. And in the Middle East, be careful about praising things in your host's house. They may offer it to you as a present, and it would be impolite to refuse it!

After all, no matter where you're going, it's always a good idea to spend some time learning about the culture. Not only because it's fun to do so, but also because it's a good way to improve your travel experience.

25. What's the main theme of the article?
    (A) Gift giving around the world.
    (B) Flowers make good presents.
    (C) Say "No" to the gifts people give.
    (D) Every country has a different culture.

26. What does the word "suitable" mean in the article?
    (A) useful
    (B) appropriate
    (C) fashionable
    (D) send

27. According to the article, which of the following would be rude?
    (A) Giving your host red roses as a gift.
    (B) Not accepting a gift from your host.
    (C) Admiring things in your host's house.
    (D) Not wrapping your gift in white paper.

My name is Jane and I moved to the U.S. with my family last year. At first, I was both excited and nervous about attending high school here. But guess what? It's been a cool experience so far!

I have a different schedule at school each day, and I have to take a lot of required classes, like math, science, and English—just like in Taiwan. I also get to choose more fun classes, like art, music, cooking, and even bowling! The best thing is that my school offers a lot of activities, such as sports teams and clubs. I joined the soccer team, and I'm in great shape now. I'm also a member of the chess club, which has helped me make new friends from different grades.

Overall, I'm enjoying my new life here in the U.S., even though I sometimes miss my friends back in Taiwan. I know how lucky I am, and I'm doing my best to learn and grow.

28. What has helped Jane make friends at her new school?
    (A) Taking lots of fun classes.
    (B) Playing on the soccer team.
    (C) Joining activities outside of class.
    (D) Missing her friends back in Taiwan.

29. How does Jane feel about her life in the U.S.?
    (A) Lucky
    (B) Nervous
    (C) Unhappy
    (D) Homesick

30. What does Jane like most at her new school?
    (A) Many activates that the school offered.
    (B) Making friends from different grades.
    (C) Required classes like math and science.
    (D) Taking fun classes like cooking and bowling.

GEPT
初級模擬試題
第 4 回

04-000

第 4 回聽力測驗

聽力測驗

本測驗分四個部分，全部都是單選題，共30題，作答時間約20分鐘。作答說明為中文，印在試題冊上並經由放音機播出。

第一部分　**看圖辨義**　◀》04-001～04-006

共5題，每題請聽放音機播出題目和三個英語句子後，選出與所看到的圖畫最相符的答案。每題只播出一遍。

示範例題

你會看到

你會聽到

Look at the picture. What is the man's job?
(A) He is a painter.
(B) He is a reporter.
(C) He is a salesman

正確答案為 (C)。

聽力測驗第一部分試題從本頁開始。

Question 1

Question 2

Question 3

開始時間	
結束時間	

Question 4

Question 5

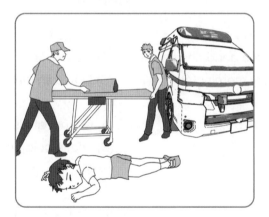

共10題，每題請聽放音機播出題目和三個英語句子後，再從試題冊上三個回答中，選出一個最適合的答案。每題只播出一遍。

示範例題

你會聽到

Does anyone know how the machine works?

你會看到

(A) Why don't you read this note?

(B) I don't know how to cook it, either.

(C) No one has to work late today.

正確答案為 (A)。

6. (A) No, it's the building on your right.
   (B) I'm not sure if this is a good choice.
   (C) Yes, I go there every morning at eight.

7. (A) Thank you for this card.
   (B) Sorry, we don't sell cars.
   (C) Sorry, we only take cash.

8. (A) I think it's Mary.
   (B) It must have been locked.
   (C) Go straight then turn right.

9. (A) I don't like it, either.
   (B) I spent hours preparing for the exam.
   (C) I'm sure you'll do better on the next test.

10. (A) I want to buy it, too.
    (B) My brother gave it to me.
    (C) It's on the shelf over there.

11. (A) So do I.
    (B) It's exciting, isn't it?
    (C) I have an idea. Let's go jogging.

12. (A) No, not at all.
    (B) That would be nice.
    (C) Yes, you are so forgiving.

13. (A) He's such a kind person.
    (B) I didn't know he owned a bike.
    (C) Did he say when he'll return it?

14. (A) I'll be downstairs right away.
    (B) No problem. I'll stay right here.
    (C) Ok. I'll go to bed in ten minutes.

15. (A) Yes, there's a convenience store on the corner.
    (B) Yes, it is. Also, it's much cheaper than taking a taxi.
    (C) The MRT is considered the best form of public transportation.

第三部分　簡短對話　◀》04-018～04-028

共10題，每題請聽放音機播出一段對話和一個相關的問題後，再從試題冊上三個選項中，選出一個最適合的答案。每段對話和問題播出一遍。

示範例題

你會聽到

（男）I can't go any faster.

（女）But the next one is at 1:40. We will be late for the test for sure.

（男）Which platform should we go to?

（女）Platform 2. It's just right near the entrance.

（男）I think we can make it in time.

Question: Where are the man and the woman?

你會看到

(A) At the airport.

(B) At the train station.

(C) In the swimming pool.

正確答案為 (B)。

16. (A) He is in a hurry.
    (B) He is on the way.
    (C) He is excited about dinner.

17. (A) A nice watch
    (B) School supplies
    (C) A pair of earrings

18. (A) She will talk to Albert.
    (B) She will punish her son.
    (C) She will call the teacher.

19. (A) He is very angry.
    (B) It's rude to be late.
    (C) They are often late.

20. (A) The man will try to lose weight.
    (B) The woman will lend her coat to the man.
    (C) The man will go to the office to get his coat.

21. (A) It's not going to be easy.
    (B) The tests won't be difficult.
    (C) The man won't have to study hard.

22. (A) He is lying.
    (B) He spent a lot of money.
    (C) He enjoys his new hobby.

23. (A) She can't make bread.
    (B) She just had a big lunch.
    (C) She doesn't eat breakfast.

24. (A) The fish tank was too dirty.
    (B) The girl gave them too much food.
    (C) The girl didn't give them enough food.

25. (A) The man will repair the vending machine.
    (B) The woman will borrow tissue paper from the man.
    (C) The woman will buy tissue paper from the machine.

第四部分 短文聽解 ◀» 04-029～04-034

共5題，每題有三個圖片選項。請聽放音機播出的題目，並選一個最適合的圖片。每題播出一遍。

示範例題

你會看到

(A)

Mon	Tue	Wed	Thur.	Fri.	Sat.	Sun.

(B)

Mon	Tue	Wed	Thur.	Fri.	Sat.	Sun.

(C)

Mon	Tue	Wed	Thur.	Fri.	Sat.	Sun.

你會聽到

Listen to the weather forecast. What's the weather like next week?

This is Good Day weather forecast. It's been hot these days. Are you worried whether it is going to be this hot next week? Then, there is good news for you. We are going to have rain for three days next week which is going to bring down the temperature a little bit. Thursday and Friday are cloudy. And we can expect clear days on the weekends.

正確答案為 (A)。

Question 26

(A)

(B)

(C)

Question 27

(A)

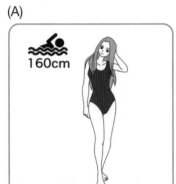

(B)

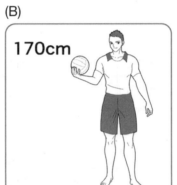

(C)

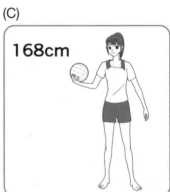

Question 28

(A)

(B)

(C)

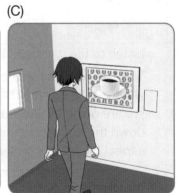

Question 29

(A)

(B)

(C)

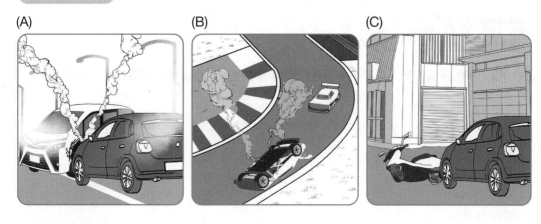

Question 30

(A)

(B)

(C)

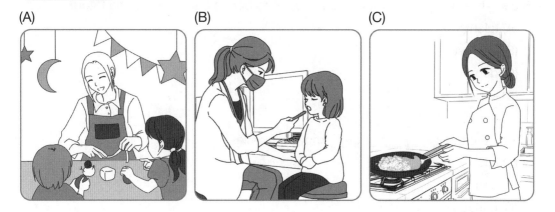

本測驗分三部分，全部都是單選題，共30題，作答時間35分鐘。

第一部分　詞彙

共10題，每個題目裡有一個空格。請從四個選項中選出一個最適合題意的字或詞作答。

1. Alex was _____ to work for several months after the car accident.
   (A) willing
   (B) unable
   (C) difficult
   (D) painful

2. Jerry has a _____ for art and hopes to become a painter in the future.
   (A) talent
   (B) interest
   (C) degree
   (D) expert

3. Tim, the most _____ guy I know, never lies.
   (A) bitter
   (B) honest
   (C) curious
   (D) childish

4. I've lost one of the _____ from my shirt.
   (A) colors
   (B) clothes
   (C) irons
   (D) buttons

5. Give me your _____ on which job offer I should accept.
   (A) record
   (B) belief
   (C) opinion
   (D) result

開始時間

結束時間

6. Can you pick Mr. Chen up when his _____ arrives?
   (A) television
   (B) napkin
   (C) package
   (D) flight

7. We need to buy some new chairs and desks, so where is the nearest _____ store?
   (A) grocery
   (B) clothing
   (C) sports
   (D) furniture

8. Benjamin asked me if I can _____ him my bike.
   (A) race
   (B) borrow
   (C) lend
   (D) repair

9. Please get the first ten items on the _____ , and I'll get the rest.
   (A) list
   (B) wrist
   (C) ink
   (D) mall

10. All the new buildings and the convenient MRT system have turned this into a _____ city.
    (A) novel
    (B) ordinary
    (C) traditional
    (D) modern

共8題，包括二個段落，每個段落含四個空格。每格均有四個選項，請依照文意選出最適合的答案。

Questions 11-14

Uncle Jerry is ____(11)____ I greatly admire. He was raised by his grandparents in a family that lacked money. From a young age, he ____(12)____ working to help support his family. Because of his humble background, he has always ____(13)____ fight for the things he desires. ____(14)____ he has faced many difficulties in his work and life, he never gives up. Uncle Jerry really inspires me with his strong will and desire to succeed.

11. (A) person   (B) someone   (C) adult   (D) character

12. (A) starts   (B) will start   (C) started   (D) has started

13. (A) has to   (B) having to   (C) have to   (D) had to

14. (A) Although   (B) Besides   (C) Even   (D) However

Questions 15-18

Clocks can not only tell time ___(15)___ beautiful sounds. A cuckoo clock is a type of clock that makes sounds like a cuckoo call when it strikes the hours. It is unknown who ___(16)___ the first cuckoo clock, but it is widely believed that the first cuckoo clocks came from the Black Forest region in southwestern Germany. Cuckoo clocks are made ___(17)___ wood and are usually decorated with leaves and animals. They come in many different designs and sizes, but they have one thing in ___(18)___ —a cuckoo bird, which sings every hour on the hour. It is one of the most popular souvenirs for people who travel to Germany.

15. (A) but also produce (B) and produce
    (C) and it produces (D) but producing

16. (A) creates (B) invented (C) has developed (D) had made

17. (A) in (B) for (C) of (D) from

18. (A) similar (B) same (C) common (D) general

共12題，包括4個題組，每個題組含1至2篇短文，與數個相關的四選一的選擇題。請由試題上的選項中選出最適合的答案。

Questions 19-21

Dear students,

As you all know, we're going to have a hot pot party at school this Saturday. As you can see on the list below, the food has been divided into different types. I'd like everyone to bring one food item of each type to the party. Your parents should be able to find all of these items at the supermarket or wet market.

Please use the list to tell me what you'd like to bring. Just sign your name next to the items you've chosen. Be sure to return the list to me by e-mail tomorrow. If there are too many of some items and not enough of others, we can make changes as needed. I'll provide you with the final list of what everyone should bring on Friday. Sauces will be available at the party, but you can also bring your own if you like.

Meat	Vegetables	Others
chicken slices _____	cabbage _____	pork balls _____
pork slices _____	lettuce _____	dumplings _____
beef slices _____	broccoli _____	shrimp _____
lamb slices _____	mushrooms _____	tofu _____
	corn _____	noodles _____

19. How many food items should each student bring to the party?
    (A) one   (B) two   (C) three   (D) four

20. What are the students asked to do?
    (A) Have their parents sign the list and return it to the teacher by e-mail.
    (B) Write a number next to each item to show how much they're bringing.
    (C) Complete the list and hand it in to the teacher on Friday.
    (D) Write their name on the list next to the food they want to bring.

21. Which of the following is true?
    (A) The teacher asks the students to buy food at the supermarket.
    (B) A hot pot party will be held at the school next Sunday.
    (C) The students won't know for sure what to bring until Friday.
    (D) The students are required to bring their own hot pot sauces.

Tired of taking the bus? Do you want a scooter, but can't afford to purchase a new one? We have all kinds of second hand scooters for you to choose from. You'll find our shop on the first floor of Metro Mall. Come have a look and take your pick! Our mechanics make sure all the scooters we sell are in good condition. We're having a special Chinese New Year sale, so now is the perfect time. Buy any used scooter and get $1,000 off. And you can get another $500 off if you spend over $20,000. This offer is only available on the two weekends before the Chinese New Year holiday.

22. If you purchase a $25,000 scooter during the sale, how much can you save?
    (A) $500
    (B) $1,000
    (C) $1,500
    (D) $2,000

23. How long will the sale last?
    (A) One day
    (B) Two days
    (C) Four days
    (D) The whole Chinese New Year holiday

24. Who would be interested in this advertisement?
    (A) A person who is interested in buying a new scooter.
    (B) Someone who doesn't like taking public transportation.
    (C) A person who wants to trade in their old scooter for a new one.
    (D) Someone who purchased a scooter and needs it repaired.

Let's have salad!

Salad makes a perfect lunch for a hot summer day. If you're tired of meat, rice, and noodles, and would like to have something a little lighter, why not try this healthy vegetarian salad **recipe**?

Ingredients:

¼ cup olive oil

½ teaspoon salt

1 ¼ cups chopped lettuce

½ cup chopped red cabbage

1 cup sliced tomatoes

¼ cup mozzarella cheese

fresh basil leaves

balsamic vinegar to taste

Time to make your salad! Put the oil, vinegar, and salt in a large bowl and mix well with a fork. Add the cabbage, tomatoes, mozzarella cheese, some basil leaves to it. Viola! Now you have a wonderful summer salad to enjoy.

25. What is a "recipe"?

(A) Something that tells you how to eat healthy.

(B) A list telling you what to buy at the supermarket.

(C) A set of steps showing you how to prepare food.

(D) Information about how you can lose weight.

26. Which of the following is true about the salad?

    (A) It will be satisfying to meat lovers.

    (B) It is for someone who likes sweets.

    (C) It will take people an hour to make.

    (D) It can be made without a stove.

27. What is probably required to make the salad but not mentioned?

    (A) a knife

    (B) a spoon

    (C) a fork

    (D) a mixer

Questions 28-30

Do your eyes feel tired after using your phone or computer? If you're looking for something that can improve your eye health, lutein may be just the thing you need. What is lutein? Many people have never heard of it. Lutein is a natural part of the human diet and is best known for its ability to improve and maintain eye health. It can be found in yellow and green fruits and vegetables. It's easier for your body to use when it's taken with a healthy fat like olive oil. As for the amount, most doctors would suggest taking 3 to 20 mg daily. According to some research, it can be good not only for eye health but also your heart and even your brain. Lutein is sold in bottles, but you can also get enough of it by eating plenty of fruits and vegetables. So next time when you see some "greens and yellows" on the dining table, be sure to eat more!

28. Which of the following is the best title for this article?
    (A) *The Right Amount of Lutein*
    (B) *The Key to a Healthy Diet*
    (C) *Stay Away from Your Screens*
    (D) *A Secret for Your Eye Health*

29. What is "lutein"?
    (A) A kind of green and yellow vegetable.
    (B) A type of fat that's good for your health.
    (C) Something found in certain vegetables.
    (D) Something that can help us lose weight.

30. Which of the following is true about lutein?
    (A) Doctors say it's still not clear what lutein can do for our health.
    (B) Some doctors don't believe it's a good idea to take it every day.
    (C) Eating fruits and vegetables isn't the only way to get enough of it.
    (D) Lutein can work better when it's taken with a lot of warm water.

GEPT
初級模擬試題
第 5 回

05-000

第 5 回聽力測驗

聽力測驗

本測驗分四個部分,全部都是單選題,共30題,作答時間約20分鐘。作答說明為中文,印在試題冊上並經由放音機播出。

第一部分 **看圖辨義** 🔊 05-001～05-006

共5題,每題請聽放音機播出題目和三個英語句子後,選出與所看到的圖畫最相符的答案。每題只播出一遍。

示範例題

你會看到

你會聽到

Look at the picture. What is the man's job?
(A) He is a painter.
(B) He is a reporter.
(C) He is a salesman

正確答案為 (C)。

聽力測驗第一部分試題從本頁開始。

Question 1

Question 2

Question 3

開始時間

結束時間

Question 4

Question 5

共10題，每題請聽放音機播出題目和三個英語句子後，再從試題冊上三個回答中，選出一個最適合的答案。每題只播出一遍。

示範例題

你會聽到

Does anyone know how the machine works?

你會看到

(A) Why don't you read this note?

(B) I don't know how to cook it, either.

(C) No one has to work late today.

正確答案為 (A)。

6. (A) Is it better now?
   (B) Really? I am, too.
   (C) Did you take the pill I gave you?

7. (A) Hi, this is Tina.
   (B) That's my cousin.
   (C) Hmm, let me guess.

8. (A) I am still thinking about it.
   (B) You can do it alone, then?
   (C) You won't know unless you try.

9. (A) I missed my flight.
   (B) When are you leaving?
   (C) I'm really sorry about that.

10. (A) Yes, I want this one.
    (B) I'd like the strawberry one.
    (C) Chocolate and strawberry are tasty.

11. (A) I don't need it.
    (B) Help would be nice.
    (C) I'm looking for a jacket.

12. (A) So have I. It was lots of fun.
    (B) No, I haven't. I used to work there.
    (C) Yes, I have. I went there last month.

13. (A) It's used to hold water.
    (B) We use it in the morning.
    (C) I used to cook for myself.

14. (A) I wouldn't do that.
    (B) Sorry, I didn't know.
    (C) No, thank you. I'm fine.

15. (A) Don't let the stranger in.
    (B) Could you please keep quiet?
    (C) You should take it to the repair shop.

第三部分　簡短對話　◀》05-018～05-028

共10題，每題請聽放音機播出一段對話和一個相關的問題後，再從試題冊上三個選項中，選出一個最適合的答案。每段對話和問題播出一遍。

示範例題

你會聽到

（男）I can't go any faster.

（女）But the next one is at 1:40. We will be late for the test for sure.

（男）Which platform should we go to?

（女）Platform 2. It's just right near the entrance.

（男）I think we can make it in time.

Question: Where are the man and the woman?

你會看到

(A) At the airport.

(B) At the train station.

(C) In the swimming pool.

正確答案為 (B)。

16. (A) She doesn't have to go.
    (B) Someone else sets up the tents.
    (C) Learning to set up a tent is difficult.

17. (A) Learn how to sing.
    (B) Listen to the radio.
    (C) Listen to rock music.

18. (A) We don't know.
    (B) It's on the table.
    (C) It's in the drugstore.

19. (A) He's a goldfish.
    (B) He's a pet dog.
    (C) He's the woman's brother.

20. (A) She will forgive her mom.
    (B) She will be honest with her mom.
    (C) She will call her mom and tell her everything.

21. (A) See his old friends.
    (B) Look for good restaurants.
    (C) Take his friends to America.

22. (A) Take a trip.
    (B) Buy a ticket
    (C) See a concert.

23. (A) They're eating.
    (B) They're cooking a meal.
    (C) They're looking at a menu.

24. (A) Sharing secrets.
    (B) Watching videos.
    (C) Learning languages.

25. (A) An exercise class.
    (B) A swimming event.
    (C) A long-distance race.

第四部分　短文聽解　◀)) 05-029～05-034

共5題，每題有三個圖片選項。請聽放音機播出的題目，並選一個最適合的圖片。每題播出一遍。

示範例題

你會看到

(A)

Mon	Tue	Wed	Thur.	Fri.	Sat.	Sun.
⛈	🌧	🌧	⛅	⛅	☀	☀

(B)

Mon	Tue	Wed	Thur.	Fri.	Sat.	Sun.
⛈	🌧	🌧	⛅	⛅	⛅	⛅

(C)

Mon	Tue	Wed	Thur.	Fri.	Sat.	Sun.
⛈	🌧	☀	☀	☀	☀	☀

你會聽到

Listen to the weather forecast. What's the weather like next week?

This is Good Day weather forecast. It's been hot these days. Are you worried whether it is going to be this hot next week? Then, there is good news for you. We are going to have rain for three days next week which is going to bring down the temperature a little bit. Thursday and Friday are cloudy. And we can expect clear days on the weekends.

正確答案為 (A)。

Question 26

(A)

(B)

(C)

Question 27

(A)

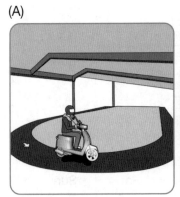

(B)

(C)

Question 28

(A)

(B)

(C)

Question 29

(A)

(B)

(C)

Question 30

(A)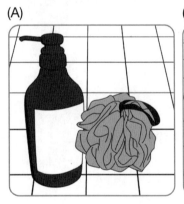

(B)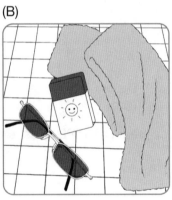

(C)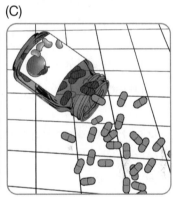

閱讀測驗

本測驗分三部分，全部都是單選題，共30題，作答時間35分鐘。

第一部分　詞彙

共10題，每個題目裡有一個空格。請從四個選項中選出一個最適合題意的字或詞作答。

1. I don't want to be late for my exam tomorrow, so can I borrow your _____ ?
   (A) scooter
   (B) balloon
   (C) wallet
   (D) textbook

2. I think we're lost; let's ask someone for _____ .
   (A) advice
   (B) money
   (C) information
   (D) directions

3. Miss Fisher often buys us ice cream after PE class; she's very _____ .
   (A) confident
   (B) hungry
   (C) generous
   (D) natural

4. I haven't _____ Betty today yet.
   (A) looked
   (B) watched
   (C) seen
   (D) heard

5. Are you Jack or Jason? Sorry, I have a poor _____ for names.
   (A) sight
   (B) speech
   (C) brain
   (D) memory

6. I hate driving to work in bad weather, so luckily it _____ snows here.
   (A) seldom
   (B) sometimes
   (C) suddenly
   (D) usually

7. I _____ chocolate ice cream, but they only had vanilla at the grocery store.
   (A) choose
   (B) prefer
   (C) admire
   (D) purchase

8. My parents punished me after I got in _____ at school.
   (A) touch
   (B) shape
   (C) trouble
   (D) line

9. Do you have anything in _____ for next week's science project?
   (A) mind
   (B) head
   (C) thought
   (D) idea

10. During the _____ season, people celebrate by giving each other gifts.
    (A) vacation
    (B) sports
    (C) holiday
    (D) business

共8題，包括二個段落，每個段落含四個空格。每格均有四個選項，請依照文意選出最適合的答案。

Questions 11-14

Come visit Nature's Wonderland, our exciting wild animal park! See lions, tigers, bears, monkeys, and more up close from your car as you ___(11)___ slowly through the park. Learn fun facts about the animals from signs along the trail. Picnic areas are available ___(12)___ you can eat lunch while watching the active animals play. Nature's Wonderland is open every day ___(13)___ 9 am to 5 pm. Tickets are $12 for adults and $8 for children under 12. A wonderful experience is waiting for nature lovers of ___(14)___ ages at Nature's Wonderland wild animal park!

11. (A) drives   (B) driven   (C) driving   (D) drive

12. (A) so   (B) and   (C) thus   (D) even

13. (A) until   (B) from   (C) at   (D) for

14. (A) every   (B) all   (C) each   (D) many

Questions 15-18

What do you do when you have free time? Some people exercise to stay healthy when they have the time, and ___(15)___ like learning new things. It doesn't really matter what you do ___(16)___ you plan your time well and find activities you really enjoy. If you aren't effective in planning your time, ___(17)___ , having a lot of time on your hands isn't necessarily a good thing. A good example is summer vacation, which last two months. If you don't use this time wisely, it's easy to become bored. In short, if you want to enjoy your free time, it's a good idea ___(18)___ a plan.

15. (A) another　　　(B) the other　　　(C) others　　　(D) together

16. (A) as long as　　(B) even though　　(C) in order to　　(D) because of

17. (A) then　　　　(B) therefore　　　(C) but　　　　(D) however

18. (A) for having　　(B) to have　　　(C) will have　　(D) that one has

共12題，包括4個題組，每個題組含1至2篇短文，與數個相關的四選一的選擇題。請由試題上的選項中選出最適合的答案。

Questions 19-21

Hi Helen,

I'm writing this email to ask if you can do me a favor. As you know, we're having a party at the office this Sunday (Jan. 26). I'm inviting some of our biggest and most important customers, so I want to have the office cleaned this Saturday. And because Irene and Sophie said that they saw a mouse in the kitchen, I want to have the job done by a cleaning company. Could you make the arrangements for me?

At the end of this email is a list of the prices charged by different cleaning services. Please have a look and choose the company that has the lowest prices and is available when we need them. We have two floors that need cleaning with three rooms and one bathroom each. Most importantly, all the companies require that you contact them at least two days before cleaning, so be sure to make the arrangements before you leave the office today. This way, the cleaners can come the day after tomorrow. Thanks in advance!

Yours,

Jim

List of cleaning service prices

Company	Per room	Per bathroom	Notes
EZ Cleaning	$1,800	$400	
Acme Cleaners	$1,500	$500	Not available until February 20, 2025
Jiffy Clean	$1,600	$600	
Honest Cleaning	$1,700	$500	

19. What will Helen have to do after receiving the email?
    (A) She will send out invitation cards.
    (B) She will start cleaning the office.
    (C) She will call Jim about the service.
    (D) She will arrange a cleaning service.

20. Which company will be hired for the job?
    (A) EZ Cleaning
    (B) Acme Cleaners
    (C) Jiffy Clean
    (D) Honest Cleaning

21. What day was the email sent on?
    (A) Wednesday
    (B) Thursday
    (C) Friday
    (D) Saturday

Smiling is a simple way to express happiness, and it benefits not only the people who smile, but also the people around them. People always wonder what they can do to improve their lives. Why not start by smiling?

People smile when they feel happy. However, many people aren't aware that smiling can actually make them feel better or help them stay calm in stressful situations. **Believe it or not**, scientists have found that even a fake smile can have a positive effect on people's mood. This is because smiling causes muscles in the face to send signals to the brain that tell people to be happy. Smiling may seem like an easy thing to do, but it can make a big difference. So don't forget to smile!

22. What is the best title for the article?
    (A) *Laughing at Others*
    (B) *The Power of Smiles*
    (C) *How to Smile Better*
    (D) *Don't Give a Fake Smile*

23. According to the article, what should we do to make a difference?
    (A) Tell people to be happy.
    (B) Make people feel better.
    (C) Remember to smile more.
    (D) Stay calm in stressful situations.

24. When do we use "believe it or not"?
    (A) When we say something surprising.
    (B) When someone is telling a lie.
    (C) When a person doesn't believe you.
    (D) When someone is being fooled.

Questions 25-27

Suzie's Garden Reopening!

After closing for three months, we're back with a new café that serves delicious drinks and <u>one-of-a-kind</u> desserts. We're celebrating our reopening with special offers only available this weekend. If you've visited us before, you'll be excited to see all the changes we've made. And if you've never been here before, you'll be surprised how happy and relaxed flowers can make you. According to research, plants are not only able to calm people down, but also bring feelings of peace. So come to Suzie's Garden, where you can spend a relaxing afternoon enjoying the beauty of flowers. We now even offer potted flowers for sale so you can enjoy them at home. If you don't want to take flowers home in a pot, how about in your stomach? We're now offering special desserts made with flowers!

Tickets

Adults: $200

Students: $120

Children 6 and under: free of charge

Potted Flowers

Lilies: $120

White roses: $200, Roses in other colors: $300

Tulips: $320

Sunflowers: $100

*With every $500 spent on tickets, receive $100 off on potted flowers

Desserts

Rose Jelly: $70

Lily cake: $120

Sunflower ice cream: $90

Tulip cookies: $60/bag $180/box

25. Who would be interested in this ad?

(A) Someone who wants to have a full meal at a café.

(B) People who want to learn to cook with flowers.

(C) Someone who wants to bring some flowers home.

(D) People who are interested in planting a garden.

26. Richard is going to take his wife, his son, who is 13, and his 5-year-old nephew wife's to Susi's garden and bring two pots of pink roses home. How much money does he need to spend?

    (A) $920

    (B) $1,020

    (C) $1,220

    (D) $1240

27. What does "one-of-a-kind" likely mean?

    (A) unique

    (B) common

    (C) fancy

    (D) different

Questions 28-30

There are many wonderful places in the world worth visiting, and Cappadocia in central Turkey is certainly one of them. It's nothing like anywhere you've ever been before. We have a day tour planned for you, and we promise the sights will amaze you.

You will be picked up in front of the hotel by our tour bus after breakfast. The first stop is Devrent Valley, which is known for its many giant rocks shaped like animals. You can see rocks that look like snakes, seals, birds, and even camels! Next stop is an art center, where you can see how traditional art and jewelry in the Cappadocia region was made. Then, you're going to dine at a fine restaurant which offers traditional Turkish food.

After the lunch break, you'll be going to Goreme Valley to see the Open Air Museum, which has ancient churches in caves with colorful paintings. Finally, you will visit the largest and deepest underground city in Cappadocia. Our tour guide will help you discover the wonders and history of this amazing place.

28. Who is most likely the author?
    (A) a tour guide
    (B) a hotel manager
    (C) a history teacher
    (D) a restaurant chef

29. What is Devrent Valley famous for?
    (A) wild animals
    (B) giant rocks
    (C) art and jewelry
    (D) fine dining

30. According to the text, which is true about Cappadocia?
    (A) It is a large ancient city in Turkey.
    (B) It has been discovered quite recently.
    (C) It is famous for its many wild animals.
    (D) It has both natural and historic sights.

GEPT
初級模擬試題
第 6 回

06-000

第 6 回聽力測驗

聽力測驗

本測驗分四個部分，全部都是單選題，共30題，作答時間約20分鐘。作答說明為中文，印在試題冊上並經由放音機播出。

第一部分　看圖辨義　◀)) 06-001～06-006

共5題，每題請聽放音機播出題目和三個英語句子後，選出與所看到的圖畫最相符的答案。每題只播出一遍。

示範例題

你會看到

你會聽到

Look at the picture. What is the man's job?
(A) He is a painter.
(B) He is a reporter.
(C) He is a salesman

正確答案為 (C)。

聽力測驗

聽力測驗第一部分試題從本頁開始。

Question 1

Question 2

Question 3

開始時間	
結束時間	

Question 4

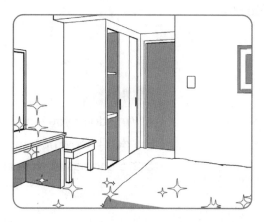

Question 5

共10題，每題請聽放音機播出題目和三個英語句子後，再從試題冊上三個回答中，選出一個最適合的答案。每題只播出一遍。

示範例題

你會聽到

Does anyone know how the machine works?

你會看到

(A) Why don't you read this note?

(B) I don't know how to cook it, either.

(C) No one has to work late today.

正確答案為 (A)。

---

6. (A) Yes, he eats a lot of it.
   (B) Let's get some for him.
   (C) I seldom have it either.

7. (A) Sure. Let me help.
   (B) No. It's my pleasure.
   (C) Yes, I opened the door.

8. (A) It takes around five minutes.
   (B) How many letters do you have?
   (C) It's across from the train station.

9. (A) Jonathan is my cousin.
   (B) He's on a trip to Japan.
   (C) Yes, he often arrives late.

10. (A) Yes, I enjoy playing tennis.
    (B) I'm not used to getting up early.
    (C) Having good habits is important.

11. (A) I can get back home before you do.
    (B) I'll leave everything at my mom's office.
    (C) What time do you want me to be there?

12. (A) When are we going to start?
    (B) All right, I'll stop doing it now.
    (C) I've never seen them in the city.

13. (A) Why do you like it?
    (B) Do you have a fever?
    (C) Let me call the police.

14. (A) I got a bad score too.
    (B) The fish isn't fresh either.
    (C) Yes, the restroom is dirty.

15. (A) Why? Are you thinking of going?
    (B) It's good to spend time with family.
    (C) I have no idea what the test is about.

第三部分　簡短對話　　🔊 06-018～06-028

共10題，每題請聽放音機播出一段對話和一個相關的問題後，再從試題冊上三個選項中，選出一個最適合的答案。每段對話和問題播出一遍。

示範例題

你會聽到

（男）I can't go any faster.

（女）But the next one is at 1:40. We will be late for the test for sure.

（男）Which platform should we go to?

（女）Platform 2. It's just right near the entrance.

（男）I think we can make it in time.

Question: Where are the man and the woman?

你會看到

(A) At the airport.

(B) At the train station.

(C) In the swimming pool.

正確答案為 (B)。

16. (A) They went to the same restaurant.
    (B) They met each other at a coffee shop.
    (C) They both spent an hour waiting in line.

17. (A) Ask the woman to lend him her notes.
    (B) Ask the woman to take the test for him.
    (C) Ask the woman to take the class with him.

18. (A) The woman is lying.
    (B) The man is being funny.
    (C) The woman has to see a doctor.

19. (A) See a doctor.
    (B) Get some food.
    (C) Go to the hospital.

20. (A) The man believes Jenny's opinion is correct.
    (B) The man doesn't agree with what Jenny said.
    (C) He doesn't think the women should have fought.

21. (A) The man's telephone was broken.
    (B) The phone's volume was turned down.
    (C) The man and woman talked on the phone.

22. (A) Go on a trip.
    (B) Check the weather.
    (C) Watch some TV shows.

23. (A) Learning to bake.
    (B) Shopping for a cake.
    (C) Looking for the man.

24. (A) They enjoy chatting with relatives.
    (B) Both of them like Chinese New Year.
    (C) Receiving lucky money is the fun part.

25. (A) He doesn't like eating snacks.
    (B) Exercising regularly is important.
    (C) The woman needs to lose weight.

第四部分 　短文聽解　◀》06-029～06-034

共5題，每題有三個圖片選項。請聽放音機播出的題目，並選一個最適合的圖片。每題播出一遍。

示範例題

你會看到

(A)

Mon	Tue	Wed	Thur.	Fri.	Sat.	Sun.
🌧	🌧	🌧	🌤	🌤	☀	☀

(B)

Mon	Tue	Wed	Thur.	Fri.	Sat.	Sun.
⛈	🌧	🌧	🌤	🌤	🌤	🌤

(C)

Mon	Tue	Wed	Thur.	Fri.	Sat.	Sun.
⛈	🌧	☀	☀	☀	☀	☀

你會聽到

Listen to the weather forecast. What's the weather like next week?

This is Good Day weather forecast. It's been hot these days. Are you worried whether it is going to be this hot next week? Then, there is good news for you. We are going to have rain for three days next week which is going to bring down the temperature a little bit. Thursday and Friday are cloudy. And we can expect clear days on the weekends.

正確答案為 (A)。

Question 26

(A)

(B)

(C)

Question 27

(A)

(B)

(C)

Question 28

(A)

(B)

(C)

Question 29

(A)
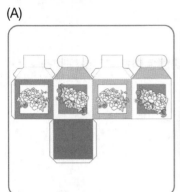

(B)
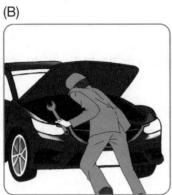

(C)
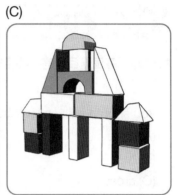

Question 30

(A)

(B)
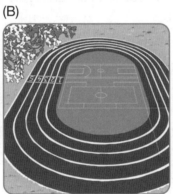

(C)
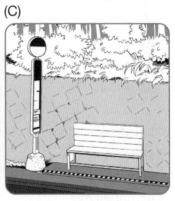

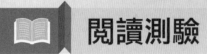

閱讀測驗

本測驗分三部分，全部都是單選題，共30題，作答時間35分鐘。

第一部分　詞彙

共10題，每個題目裡有一個空格。請從四個選項中選出一個最適合題意的字或詞作答。

1. You should always look both ways before you _____ the street.
   (A) drive
   (B) turn
   (C) cross
   (D) walk

2. Roger is very _____ . He doesn't care about his friends and family.
   (A) greedy
   (B) warm
   (C) jealous
   (D) selfish

3. I marked my doctor's visit on the _____ so I wouldn't forget to go.
   (A) memory
   (B) program
   (C) notebook
   (D) calendar

4. I have no _____ after cleaning the whole house from top to bottom.
   (A) energy
   (B) motion
   (C) youth
   (D) waste

5. Please put the flowers in a _____ and don't forget to add some water.
   (A) lamp
   (B) vase
   (C) course
   (D) napkin

6. My dad always drinks black coffee, but it's too _____ for me.
   (A) sweet
   (B) spicy
   (C) bitter
   (D) thick

7. Jane said she would _____ for my birthday party, but she never came.
   (A) wake up
   (B) get up
   (C) dress up
   (D) show up

8. The swimming pool is only available for use by club _____ .
   (A) members
   (B) passengers
   (C) servants
   (D) individuals

9. Traffic was heavy this morning, so it took me _____ to get to work than usual.
   (A) longer
   (B) slower
   (C) quicker
   (D) faster

10. My parents are going to Thailand for vacation this year, but I won't be _____ them.
    (A) inventing
    (B) joining
    (C) booking
    (D) reminding

共8題，包括二個段落，每個段落含四個空格。每格均有四個選項，請依照文意選出最適合的答案。

Questions 11-14

When I was a high school student, I always struggled with math. It was my _____(11)_____ subject in school, and I always had trouble understanding it. However, I never gave up and kept _____(12)_____ . Miss Miller was very patient and always encouraged me. She _____(13)_____ me that it's all right to make mistakes and that's how we learn. She helped me become more confident and I slowly started to improve. Miss Miller was the first person _____(14)_____ my interest in math.

11. (A) strongest   (B) hardest   (C) weakest   (D) easiest

12. (A) considering   (B) solving   (C) practicing   (D) swallowing

13. (A) talked   (B) told   (C) said   (D) spoke

14. (A) inspired   (B) that inspire   (C) would inspire   (D) to inspire

Questions 15-18

Karen was so ___(15)___ with her cousin, Eric. She asked him to take care of her cat while she was away ___(16)___ a trip, but he forgot to feed it. When she came back, her cat was very skinny and sick. Karen was so angry ___(17)___ she didn't want to talk to Eric. However, Eric felt really bad and decided to do ___(18)___ to make up for it. So he bought Karen a new bed for her cat. Karen was very surprised and happy. She forgave Eric and thanked him for the gift.

15. (A) angry   (B) happy   (C) sad   (D) surprised

16. (A) in   (B) on   (C) at   (D) by

17. (A) when   (B) that   (C) then   (D) while

18. (A) nothing   (B) everything   (C) something   (D) anything

共12題，包括4個題組，每個題組含1至2篇短文，與數個相關的四選一的選擇題。請由試題上的選項中選出最適合的答案。

Questions 19-21

Subject: Welcome to Our New Factory!
Dec 10, 2024

Dear Team,

Exciting news! Our new factory opened on December 9, 2024!

I know you can't wait to work in the newly-completed sports equipment factory. I can't either, and I will give you a tour of our new factory at 2 p.m. tomorrow. However, before the tour, please read the warning notice that is posted outside of the factory entrance. Be sure to obey all the safety rules when inside the factory. Thank you for your attention.

Let's make our new factory safe and successful!

Best regards,

Frank Smith
Factory Manager

Warning Notice

*No running inside the factory.

*Always wear a helmet and gloves for protection.

*Read the handbook before operating any machine, and make sure you follow
 each step in the handbook.

*Don't touch any machine you don't know how to operate.

*Press the emergency button if anything goes wrong.

---

19. What's the main purpose of Frank Smith's email?

    (A) To introduce the team's new members.

    (B) To share the launch date with his team.

    (C) To tell the workers about a factory tour.

    (D) To ask team members to read a notice.

20. Who is the email for?

    (A) Other managers

    (B) All office workers

    (C) New factory workers

    (D) Sports team members

21. According to the warning notice, what is true about working in the factory?

    (A) Workers can skip a few steps in order to speed things up.

    (B) Helmets and gloves can keep workers from all dangers.

    (C) People can only operate machines they know how to use.

    (D) Experienced workers aren't required to read the handbook.

Westminster, a busy area in London, is home to Buckingham Palace. Another famous sight is the Palace of Westminster, where you'll find Elizabeth Tower, better known as **Big Ben**. The chime of the bells in this clock tower can be heard from miles away. Just west of the palace is Westminster Abbey, a historic church where many English kings and queens have been crowned. In addition to sights like the Abbey, Westminster also has many museums, theaters, art galleries and restaurants for visitors to enjoy. It truly has something for everyone. And to the north, not far from Westminster, is Oxford Street, which is known as Europe's busiest shopping street. If you ever come to London, make sure to pay a visit to Westminster!

22. What is Big Ben?
    (A) A clock
    (B) A tower
    (C) A church
    (D) A chime

23. What can visitors do at Westminster Abby?
    (A) Have a nice dinner.
    (B) Watch a play.
    (C) Learn about history.
    (D) Do some shopping.

24. Which would be the best title for this article?
    (A) *Westminster, Europe's Busiest Shopping*
    (B) *Westminster, Something for Everyone*
    (C) *The Historic Palace of Westminster*
    (D) *Westminster, Home of Kings and Queens*

Questions 25-27

Do you know that the liver, one of our body's most important organs, has an amazing ability to regrow? When the liver gets hurt or a part of it is taken out, it can repair itself and grow back. This ability is called liver regrowth.

The liver is made up of tiny cells called hepatocytes. These cells are like little factories that can produce new liver tissue. When the liver gets damaged, these cells start working hard to fix it. They divide and grow, gradually making the liver whole again.

The fact that our livers can regrow provides hope for people with liver disease. Understanding how the liver repairs itself could **lead to** new treatments, and possibly even the ability to create whole new livers.

25. According to the article, which is true?
    (A) Everything in our body can regrow.
    (B) You can get a new liver at the hospital.
    (C) There are factories that can make livers.
    (D) A liver can grow back when it's damaged.

26. What function of hepatocytes is mentioned?
    (A) Removing waste from the blood
    (B) Producing new liver tissue
    (C) Creating whole new livers
    (D) Curing liver disease

27. Which is closest in meaning to the phrase "lead to"?
    (A) start
    (B) cause
    (C) solve
    (D) depend

My name is Connie and I'm from Korea. I came to England to study English. I'm staying with a host family in London. I share a room with my roommate, Giorgia, who is from Italy. Giorgia makes **panna cotta** every weekend, and thanks to her, I've started to fall in love with desserts. Although Giorgia and I go to the same English language school, we're in different classes. I was placed in a higher level class because I've been studying English for over ten years. Giorgia wasn't really serious about learning English until recently.

I only have classes in the morning, but Giorgia has to stay at school until three o'clock in the afternoon. While waiting for her, I usually go to the library or the campus café. Once Giorgia finishes, we head back home together, often stopping by Tesco to buy breakfast food for the next day. We spend a lot of time together even though we don't always understand each other. I really enjoy having her as a friend. She makes this place feel like a home away from home.

28. What is panna cotta?
    (A) A drink
    (B) A pasta
    (C) A snack
    (D) A dessert

29. What do Connie and Giorgia do in the afternoon?
    (A) They go shopping at a supermarket.
    (B) They spend time studying at the library.
    (C) They both have classes in the afternoon.
    (D) They have coffee together at a coffee shop.

30. How does Connie feel about staying in England?
    (A) She misses her family and friends back in Korea.
    (B) She likes her host family and her classmates a lot.
    (C) She is happy because she has made lots of friends.
    (D) She enjoys her time there because of her roommate.

GEPT
初級模擬試題
第7回

07-000

第 7 回聽力測驗

聽力測驗

本測驗分四個部分,全部都是單選題,共30題,作答時間約20分鐘。作答説明為中文,印在試題冊上並經由放音機播出。

第一部分 **看圖辨義** ◀ 07-001〜07-006

共5題,每題請聽放音機播出題目和三個英語句子後,選出與所看到的圖畫最相符的答案。每題只播出一遍。

示範例題

你會看到

你會聽到

Look at the picture. What is the man's job?
(A) He is a painter.
(B) He is a reporter.
(C) He is a salesman

正確答案為 (C)。

聽力測驗第一部分試題從本頁開始。

Question 1

Question 2

Question 3

開始時間	
結束時間	

Question 4

Question 5

共10題，每題請聽放音機播出題目和三個英語句子後，再從試題冊上三個回答中，選出一個最適合的答案。每題只播出一遍。

示範例題

你會聽到

Does anyone know how the machine works?

你會看到

(A) Why don't you read this note?

(B) I don't know how to cook it, either.

(C) No one has to work late today.

正確答案為 (A)。

6. (A) Yes, a long time ago.
   (B) Yes, I'll read it tomorrow.
   (C) No, but I did last semester.

7. (A) On platform 2.
   (B) In five minutes.
   (C) Yes, it's coming soon.

8. (A) It was delicious.
   (B) Medium, please.
   (C) I enjoyed my stay.

9. (A) Two bags.
   (B) Twenty-five dollars.
   (C) It's expensive.

10. (A) As soon as they arrive.
    (B) It's OK. Just take turns.
    (C) Don't worry. The people can wait.

11. (A) The teacher will be late.
    (B) We watched a short film.
    (C) I think we're having a quiz.

12 (A) I didn't know she was writing a report.
    (B) Good. She'll need it right when she arrives.
    (C) Yes. It took her a month to finish the report.

13. (A) Yes, I love to work very much.
    (B) Congratulations. It's such an honor.
    (C) Thanks. It took me three months to finish.

14. (A) I don't know what time it is.
    (B) Oh, no. It's my worst subject.
    (C) Math class is at eleven o'clock.

15. (A) Well, it's a lot of work.
    (B) Sure, you can use my pen.
    (C) I told you not to pet the dog.

第三部分 簡短對話 ◀》07-018～07-028

共10題，每題請聽放音機播出一段對話和一個相關的問題後，再從試題冊上三個選項中，選出一個最適合的答案。每段對話和問題播出一遍。

示範例題

你會聽到

（男）I can't go any faster.

（女）But the next one is at 1:40. We will be late for the test for sure.

（男）Which platform should we go to?

（女）Platform 2. It's just right near the entrance.

（男）I think we can make it in time.

Question: Where are the man and the woman?

你會看到

(A) At the airport.

(B) At the train station.

(C) In the swimming pool.

___

正確答案為 (B)。

16. (A) Jessie had a stomachache.
    (B) The woman made the sandwich.
    (C) The man told Jessie not to eat it.

17. (A) Spanish is more difficult than Japanese.
    (B) The father lived in Japan for many years.
    (C) The father and daughter have the same problem.

18. (A) The reason they like their teacher.
    (B) The teaching methods Miss Ou uses.
    (C) How much they like their former teacher.

19. (A) Read a story.
    (B) Watch a movie.
    (C) Go to a movie theater.

20. (A) Her grandma visited her.
    (B) A member of her family died.
    (C) Tina doesn't like the man anymore.

21. (A) He fixed the broken chair leg.
    (B) He broke his leg on the chair.
    (C) He told the woman about a danger.

22. (A) Buy a new phone.
    (B) Keep using her phone.
    (C) Have a cheap repair done.

23. (A) The fish dishes are better than the chicken dishes.
    (B) He thinks the woman is right about the restaurant.
    (C) The woman should give the restaurant another chance.

24. (A) She'll be able to walk again.
    (B) She'll be in pain for months.
    (C) Her leg will never get better.

25. (A) She's afraid to cook dinner.
    (B) She's scared of her brother.
    (C) She isn't a good cook.

◀)) 07-029～07-034

共5題，每題有三個圖片選項。請聽放音機播出的題目，並選一個最適合的圖片。每題播出一遍。

示範例題

你會看到

(A)

Mon	Tue	Wed	Thur.	Fri.	Sat.	Sun.
🌧️	🌧️	🌧️	⛅	⛅	☀️	☀️

(B)

Mon	Tue	Wed	Thur.	Fri.	Sat.	Sun.
⛈️	🌧️	🌧️	⛅	⛅	⛅	⛅

(C)

Mon	Tue	Wed	Thur.	Fri.	Sat.	Sun.
⛈️	🌧️	☀️	☀️	☀️	☀️	☀️

你會聽到

Listen to the weather forecast. What's the weather like next week?

This is Good Day weather forecast. It's been hot these days. Are you worried whether it is going to be this hot next week? Then, there is good news for you. We are going to have rain for three days next week which is going to bring down the temperature a little bit. Thursday and Friday are cloudy. And we can expect clear days on the weekends.

正確答案為 (A)。

141

Question 26

(A)

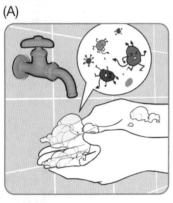

(B)

(C)

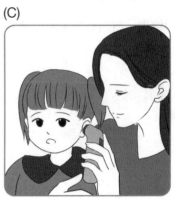

Question 27

(A)

(B)

(C)

Question 28

(A)

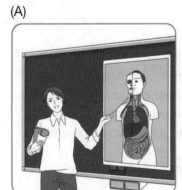

(B)

(C)

Question 29

(A)

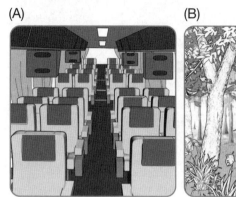

(B)

(C)

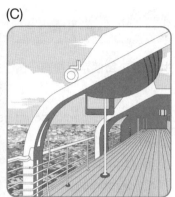

Question 30

(A)

(B)

(C)

閱讀測驗

本測驗分三部分，全部都是單選題，共30題，作答時間35分鐘。

第一部分　詞彙

共10題，每個題目裡有一個空格。請從四個選項中選出一個最適合題意的字或詞作答。

1. Small backpacks count as _____ items on most flights.
   (A) foreign
   (B) regular
   (C) personal
   (D) dangerous

2. Terry never _____ fault, nor does he apologize.
   (A) receives
   (B) obeys
   (C) believes
   (D) admits

3. If you send the letter today, it should be _____ on Wednesday.
   (A) delivered
   (B) canceled
   (C) measured
   (D) forced

4. The team celebrated their _____ after winning the basketball game.
   (A) influence
   (B) opportunity
   (C) victory
   (D) freedom

5. The _____ president was very popular, but the current president isn't.
   (A) primary
   (B) former
   (C) local
   (D) national

6. I don't feel like climbing to the top of the tower because I'm afraid of _____ .
   (A) buildings
   (B) animals
   (C) planes
   (D) heights

7. Can you _____ why you're almost two hours late?
   (A) explain
   (B) accept
   (C) notice
   (D) discuss

8. The movie was so _____ that both Eric and I fell asleep.
   (A) exciting
   (B) boring
   (C) scary
   (D) funny

9. Dora has a toothache. Would you mind taking her to see a _____ ?
   (A) vet
   (B) dentist
   (C) lawyer
   (D) doctor

10. After a long day at work, _____ of us had the energy to go out for dinner.
   (A) all
   (B) both
   (C) none
   (D) either

共8題，包括二個段落，每個段落含四個空格。每格均有四個選項，請依照文意選出最適合的答案。

Questions 11-14

Last weekend, my parents took me camping for my sixteenth birthday. It was my _____(11)_____ first camping trip. We drove a few hours from our city to a national park with a beautiful lake. When we got to our campsite, my dad _____(12)_____ the new tent he had bought for the trip, while my mom rolled out our sleeping bags. I helped by collecting sticks for our campfire later that night. My favorite part was when we cooked hot dogs over the fire and told stories under the stars. Even _____(13)_____ I was tired, I had trouble falling asleep on the bumpy ground. After a fun weekend of fishing, hiking, and exploring the outdoors, I _____(14)_____ wait for our next camping trip!

11. (A) only   (B) very   (C) single   (D) really

12. (A) set out   (B) set up   (C) put in   (D) put down

13. (A) though   (B) although   (C) then   (D) when

14. (A) don't   (B) won't   (C) can   (D) can't

Questions 15-18

In order to prepare for a swimming contest, Lisa decided to practice swimming every morning. She ___(15)___ finding a swimming pool in her neighborhood. She then ___(16)___ her swimsuit and a towel and walked to the swimming pool. When she got there, the pool appeared to be closed. She ___(17)___ the lifeguard and asked, "Excuse me, when does the pool open?" The lifeguard looked at her and said, "It's already open! You're just at the wrong entrance. This is the entrance for people who work here. Don't worry, I'll take you to the right entrance." ___(18)___ the lifeguard, Lisa found a good place to practice for the swimming contest.

15. (A) started to   (B) started by   (C) started up   (D) started on

16. (A) rented   (B) bought   (C) wore   (D) packed

17. (A) got back to   (B) came up with   (C) walked up to   (D) ran out of

18. (A) Next to   (B) Along with   (C) Thanks to   (D) Except for

共12題，包括4個題組，每個題組含1至2篇短文，與數個相關的四選一的選擇題。請由試題上的選項中選出最適合的答案。

Questions 19-21

22-year-old Ivana was one of the best athletes at her school. She used to be good at all kinds of sports, including swimming, tennis, basketball and bicycle racing. However, everything changed after she fell off her bike.

Ivana's right leg was seriously hurt in the accident, and she thought she may never be able to play her favorite sports again. After a month recovering in the hospital, she still wasn't able to walk. She told her doctor she'd do anything to be able to walk again, so her doctor gave her exercises to do to improve her strength. At first, she fell down every time she tried to get up, but she didn't give up. After two weeks, she started walking again. A month later, she left the hospital, and she was back on her bike again.

This is all because she believes in herself.

19. Which is the best title for the reading?
    (A) *Women Are Good at Sports*
    (B) *Swimming Is the Best Exercise*
    (C) *A Woman Who Never Gives up*
    (D) *The Smartest Woman in the World*

20. Where did Ivana most likely get hurt?
    (A) In a race track
    (B) On a tennis court
    (C) In a swimming pool
    (D) On a basketball court

21. After the accident, how long was it before Ivana could walk again?

(A) Four weeks

(B) Six weeks

(C) Eight weeks

(D) Ten weeks

Questions 22-24

Have you ever returned something you bought? People often return items because they are damaged, the wrong size, or the wrong color, or sometimes they simply change their minds.

If the product is damaged, you can either get your money back or get a new one. If the size or color is wrong, you can return the item and exchange it for the one you want. If you simply don't want the item, you can usually get your money back if you return it within 7 days and it's unused. You'll need to show the receipt though, so be sure to keep it.

Remember to check the store's return policy before you shop. Some stores have special rules or fees for returns. Knowing these rules can make it easier to return things.

22. Why is it important to check the store's return policy before making a purchase?

(A) To know if there's a fee for returns.

(B) To find out the different ways to pay.

(C) To know what's available at the store.

(D) To get the best price on sale items.

23. According to the article, which is NOT true?

(A) People can get a refund for a damaged item.

(B) People should keep their receipts when shopping.

(C) People can get a refund for items they don't want.

(D) People can get a refund for returns within 10 days.

24. Which of the following is the best title for this article?

   (A) *The Art of Successful Shopping*

   (B) *The Best Online Shopping Tips*

   (C) *A Guide to Returning Purchases*

   (D) *Think Twice Before You Shop*

Questions 25-27

Shadow play is the ancient art of telling stories with shadows. The history of shadow play goes back more than 2,000 years, and probably started in China. The art uses flat figures made from materials like leather, and sometimes painted in bright colors. The figures are placed between a light source and a thin white screen, which creates shadows on the screen. When the figures are moved, the shadows the audience sees move along with them. In this way, storytellers can tell interesting stories using only shadows.

Over the centuries, shadow play spread to many countries around the world. In Turkey, a form of shadow play called Karagöz began hundreds of years ago. Often held in coffee houses, the plays have funny stories with lots of singing and dancing. However, shadow play is not just for fun; it's also an important way to keep old stories and traditions alive. It's a magical way to tell stories that everyone can enjoy!

25. Which is NOT required for shadow play?

   (A) Moving shadows

   (B) Natural light

   (C) Flat figures

   (D) A thin screen

26. In shadow play, what happens when light shines on the figures?

   (A) They disappear from the screen.

   (B) They change to a different color.

   (C) They move on the screen.

   (D) They appear on the screen.

27. Why does shadow play have value as an art form?

    (A) It uses figures to make shadows.

    (B) It has many colorful characters.

    (C) It passes on stories from the past.

    (D) It comes from all over the world.

Questions 28-30

Maglev trains, or magnetic levitation trains, are a very advanced type of train system. Strong magnets on the bottom of the train and along the tracks allow these special trains to travel above the tracks instead of on them. This provides a very smooth and quiet experience for passengers.

Unlike normal trains with metal wheels that roll on tracks, maglev trains move without touching the track. This allows maglevs to reach much higher speeds—over 500 km per hour, which is faster than some airplanes. However, they do have wheels that can be used when required for safety purposes. Faster speeding up and slowing down is also possible. These advanced trains also save power and need repairs less often.

Countries including Japan, Germany and China have already introduced maglev train lines. In Japan, a maglev train reached the record speed of 603 km per hour in 2015. A number of new maglev rail lines are still being built around the world. Those who support maglev trains believe they will be the future of train travel.

28. What can we expect when riding on a maglev train?

    (A) We can enjoy a more pleasant ride.

    (B) We should allow more time to travel.

    (C) It offers great service and bigger seats.

    (D) We can travel faster than airplanes.

29. How are maglev trains different than regular trains?

   (A) They travel on wheels just like a car.

   (B) They have an electric power source.

   (C) They make use of a high speed engine.

   (D) They don't make contact with the track.

30. What do we know about the future of maglev trains?

   (A) They will be able to travel faster in a few years.

   (B) They will be made of even lighter materials.

   (C) The ticket prices can be expected to drop.

   (D) They will become more common in the world.

GEPT
初級模擬試題
第 8 回

08-000

第 8 回聽力測驗

聽力測驗

本測驗分四個部分，全部都是單選題，共30題，作答時間約20分鐘。作答說明為中文，印在試題冊上並經由放音機播出。

第 8 回

第一部分 **看圖辨義** ◀» 08-001～08-006

共5題，每題請聽放音機播出題目和三個英語句子後，選出與所看到的圖畫最相符的答案。每題只播出一遍。

示範例題

你會看到

你會聽到

Look at the picture. What is the man's job?
(A) He is a painter.
(B) He is a reporter.
(C) He is a salesman

正確答案為 (C)。

聽力測驗第一部分試題從本頁開始。

Question 1

Question 2

Question 3

開始時間	
結束時間	

Question 4

Question 5

共10題，每題請聽放音機播出題目和三個英語句子後，再從試題冊上三個回答中，選出一個最適合的答案。每題只播出一遍。

示範例題

你會聽到

Does anyone know how the machine works?

你會看到

(A) Why don't you read this note?

(B) I don't know how to cook it, either.

(C) No one has to work late today.

正確答案為 (A)。

6. (A) Stay away. It's deep.
   (B) You should see a doctor.
   (C) Let me sew it up for you.

7. (A) He's stuck in traffic.
   (B) He's always on time.
   (C) That's a good excuse.

8. (A) It's for you.
   (B) I keep coins in it
   (C) The box is empty.

9. (A) Yes. It's very old.
   (B) How did you do it?
   (C) Go put some socks on.

10. (A) Not at all.
    (B) It's OK for me.
    (C) Sure. No problem.

11. (A) I haven't seen the brush.
    (B) Would you mind doing that?
    (C) The waste will be collected today.

12. (A) It's mine, not Max's.
    (B) Your desk is fancy, too.
    (C) Because I'm really lazy.

13. (A) Where can I find it?
    (B) The wallet belongs to Irene.
    (C) Yes, but it's not the color I want.

14. (A) All right. Stand up!
    (B) Of course. What time?
    (C) You can pick up the trash.

15. (A) You can ride a bike there.
    (B) I thought I saw you there.
    (C) Come on. You still have to go.

第三部分　簡短對話　◀》08-018～08-028

共10題，每題請聽放音機播出一段對話和一個相關的問題後，再從試題冊上三個選項中，選出一個最適合的答案。每段對話和問題播出一遍。

示範例題

你會聽到

（男）I can't go any faster.

（女）But the next one is at 1:40. We will be late for the test for sure.

（男）Which platform should we go to?

（女）Platform 2. It's just right near the entrance.

（男）I think we can make it in time.

Question: Where are the man and the woman?

你會看到

(A) At the airport.

(B) At the train station.

(C) In the swimming pool.

正確答案為 (B)。

16. (A) She is upset.
    (B) She is curious.
    (C) She is confident.

17. (A) They're going to work in the yard.
    (B) They're going to plant some trees.
    (C) They're going to do some shopping.

18. (A) Lend the book to the girl.
    (B) Read the girl's story book.
    (C) Return the book to the girl.

19. (A) In a shop.
    (B) At a restaurant.
    (C) In a hotel room.

20. (A) Baking some food.
    (B) Taking something to Janet.
    (C) Driving her son somewhere.

21. (A) The man made a mistake.
    (B) The woman enjoyed her drink.
    (C) The man used too much sugar.

22. (A) The woman is new to the company.
    (B) Making calls is part of the woman's job.
    (C) The man will buy a new desk for the woman.

23. (A) The man practiced less than the woman.
    (B) The woman practiced more than the man.
    (C) The man jogged more often than the woman.

24. (A) Upstairs.
    (B) In the yard.
    (C) In the basement.

25. (A) He is going to win the prize.
    (B) He will tell the woman a secret.
    (C) He is going to talk to the woman.

第四部分　短文聽解　◀)) 08-029～08-034

共5題，每題有三個圖片選項。請聽放音機播出的題目，並選一個最適合的圖片。每題播出一遍。

示範例題

你會看到

(A)

Mon	Tue	Wed	Thur.	Fri.	Sat.	Sun.
🌧️	🌧️	🌧️	⛅	⛅	☀️	☀️

(B)

Mon	Tue	Wed	Thur.	Fri.	Sat.	Sun.
⛈️	🌧️	🌧️	⛅	⛅	⛅	⛅

(C)

Mon	Tue	Wed	Thur.	Fri.	Sat.	Sun.
⛈️	🌧️	☀️	☀️	☀️	☀️	☀️

你會聽到

Listen to the weather forecast. What's the weather like next week?

This is Good Day weather forecast. It's been hot these days. Are you worried whether it is going to be this hot next week? Then, there is good news for you. We are going to have rain for three days next week which is going to bring down the temperature a little bit. Thursday and Friday are cloudy. And we can expect clear days on the weekends.

正確答案為 (A)。

Question 26

(A)

(B)

(C)

Question 27

(A)

(B)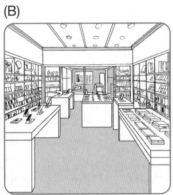

(C)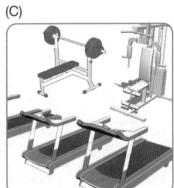

Question 28

(A)

(B)

(C)

Question 29

(A)

(B)

(C)

Question 30

(A)
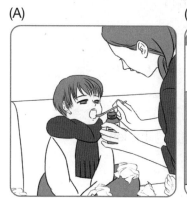

(B)
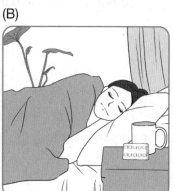

(C)

閱讀測驗

本測驗分三部分，全部都是單選題，共30題，作答時間35分鐘。

第一部分　詞彙

共10題，每個題目裡有一個空格。請從四個選項中選出一個最適合題意的字或詞作答。

1. My mom told me not to _____ my time on video games.
   (A) select
   (B) waste
   (C) divide
   (D) pass

2. The sign says wet _____ , so don't sit on the bench.
   (A) wood
   (B) metal
   (C) paint
   (D) steam

3. You'll have to buy some stamps if you want to _____ this letter.
   (A) write
   (B) receive
   (C) mail
   (D) deliver

4. Make sure that you get the car _____ before we go on our road trip.
   (A) swept
   (B) parked
   (C) driven
   (D) fixed

5. There have been a lot of _____ between Alexander and his father.
   (A) conflicts
   (B) questions
   (C) mistakes
   (D) faults

6. If you can hit the _____ , you are the winner.
   (A) target
   (B) focus
   (C) launch
   (D) meter

7. Kenny _____ cheating on the test. He promised not to do it again.
   (A) planned
   (B) forgot
   (C) regretted
   (D) enjoyed

8. Before speaking in front of others, it's good to _____ your thoughts.
   (A) underline
   (B) organize
   (C) separate
   (D) realize

9. He'd _____ listen to music than watch TV because he finds it more relaxing.
   (A) whether
   (B) better
   (C) instead
   (D) rather

10. You have so few friends because you are _____ to people.
    (A) frank
    (B) polite
    (C) rude
    (D) generous

共8題，包括二個段落，每個段落含四個空格。每格均有四個選項，請依照文意選出最適合的答案。

Questions 11-14

Samantha was very excited to start her new job as a secretary. On her first day, her manager gave her a _____(11)_____ of the office and introduced her to the other employees. Samantha was surprised to see that there were so many different _____(12)_____ in the company. Her manager then showed her how to use the phone and computer. Samantha paid careful _____(13)_____ , taking notes as he spoke. As the day went on, she began to answer phone calls and greet visitors. At the end of the day, Samantha's manager called her into his office. "You did a great job today," he said. "Keep up the good work!" It was a long, hard day, but Samantha felt proud _____(14)_____ .

11. (A) desk   (B) tour
    (C) key   (D) view

12. (A) instruments   (B) basements
    (C) apartments   (D) departments

13. (A) advice   (B) concern
    (C) attention   (D) respect

14. (A) of herself   (B) of her
    (C) in herself   (D) about her

Questions 15-18

Hiking in the mountains can be a fun experience for anyone ____(15)____ enjoys outdoor activities. However, it's important to get everything ready before you go to make sure your hike is safe and enjoyable. There are things that you need to prepare, including hiking boots, a backpack, extra clothing, and plenty of water and snacks. You should also bring a map ____(16)____ you get lost. In addition, you should always check the weather before you go. You may be run into trouble in the mountains if the weather turns bad. Finally, do not leave any trash on the trail and avoid ____(17)____ plants and wildlife. Everyone is ____(18)____ for protecting the environment.

15. (A) whom   (B) which
    (C) who   (D) whose

16. (A) even though   (B) after
    (C) until   (D) in case

17. (A) damaged   (B) damage
    (C) to damage   (D) damaging

18. (A) responsible   (B) possible
    (C) available   (D) comfortable

共12題,包括4個題組,每個題組含1至2篇短文,與數個相關的四選一的選擇題。請由試題上的選項中選出最適合的答案。

Questions 19-21

Roy

Hey, Lisa! I'm planning a birthday party for my girlfriend in September and want to get her something special.

Lisa

Cool. Do you have anything in mind?

Roy

I mentioned shoes, but she didn't seem interested. I'm thinking jewelry. Something that will go with her red dress or her favorite earrings. Are you free this afternoon?

Lisa

I'm having lunch with my dad. We'll be done by 2:00. We can meet somewhere after that.

Roy

Great! How about Metro Mall? They're having a summer sale that just started this week.

Lisa

Sounds good. I'll go there after lunch. It'll take me about an hour to get there. See you then!

Summer Sale Metro Mall July 20 - August 10		
1F	Shoes	Designer shoes: NT$5000 → NT$3000
2F	Women's clothing	Dresses: NT$5000 → NT$4000 Earrings: NT$2000 → NT$1000 Necklaces: NT$4000 → NT$3000
3F	Men's clothes	Jackets: NT$4000 → NT$3000 Pants: NT$3000 → NT$2400
4F	Sporting Goods	Baseball bat: NT$1800 → NT$1400 Basketball: NT$1500 → NT$1200

19. When are Roy and Lisa going to meet?

    (A) 12:00

    (B) 14:00

    (C) 15:00

    (D) 17:00

20. How much will Roy likely save on his girlfriend's gift?

    (A) 20%

    (B) 25%

    (C) 40%

    (D) 50%

21. What month is it now?

    (A) June

    (B) July

    (C) August

    (D) September

Countries around the world all have their own unique cultures, and with different cultures come different **superstitions**. In America, for example, it is believed by many that breaking a mirror will bring seven years of bad luck. There is also a saying in the U.S., "Step on a crack, break your mother's back." It means one should avoid stepping on cracks in the sidewalk, or it may bring bad luck for one's mother. In Thailand, there's a superstition that if a woman sings in the kitchen, she will end up marrying an old man. In Taiwan, some believe that if you point at the moon, your ear will be cut off. Another common Taiwanese superstition is that whistling late at night will bring evil spirits. Considering how big the world is, it's no surprise that people in different places have different beliefs. Many superstitions may seem silly to us, but it's best to show respect for other cultures and appreciate the differences.

22. What does the word "superstition" mean?

    (A) Things you shouldn't do because they're not legal.

    (B) Nice things to do if you want to live a happy life.

    (C) A lie that is told to make people feel scared.

    (D) Widely held beliefs that are not based on facts.

23. What is believed to happen if people break a mirror in the United States?

    (A) It will bring evil spirits or ghosts.

    (B) They'll step on cracks in the sidewalk

    (C) They'll experience years of bad luck

    (D) Bad things will happen to their mothers.

24. What do we learn from the article?

    (A) We should respect different cultures.

    (B) Being superstitious is a good thing.

    (C) We shouldn't believe superstitions.

    (D) Superstitions are common in Thailand.

Questions 25-27

I want to share my recent experience visiting my father at the hospital. My dad had to go to the hospital for a minor operation, and I went to visit him the following day. I was a little nervous because I don't like going to hospitals. But a kind volunteer helped me find my dad's room.

When I entered the room, my dad was resting, and he looked quite tired. I sat down next to him and asked him how he was feeling. He told me that he was in a lot of pain but was happy to see me. We talked about various things, and I tried to make him laugh to take his mind off the pain.

Before leaving, I talked to the nurse. I asked her how we could help my dad recover after he returned home. She gave me some helpful tips. I hugged my dad and told him I would be back soon. Even though it was tough seeing him in pain, I was glad I could be there for him and offer my support.

25. Why did the author visit the hospital?
    (A) Because he is a student of medicine.
    (B) His father was receiving treatment there.
    (C) The nurse asked him to be a volunteer.
    (D) His father had to perform an operation.

26. What did the author do at the hospital?
    (A) He tried to cheer his father up.
    (B) He gave his father medicine.
    (C) He helped his father do his work.
    (D) He took care of his dad's wound.

27. According to the article, which is true?
    (A) The author's dad is too sick to leave the hospital anytime soon.
    (B) The author got a lot of help from strangers at the hospital.
    (C) The author's father is recovering well and is able to walk around.
    (D) The author learned something useful before leaving the hospital.

Have you ever taken a ride on a hot air balloon? It's an incredible experience! You'll float high above the ground and feel like you're flying with the birds. The view from the balloon is amazing, and you can see for miles in every direction.

Before the balloon goes up, you'll receive information on safely entering the basket. Once you're in the air, the ride is smooth and peaceful. You'll feel the warmth from the burner, which is what keeps the balloon in the air.

The whole ride lasts about an hour, but it will feel like no time at all. It's a great activity to do with friends or family. If you're looking for a new experience, taking a hot air balloon ride is a must-try!

28. According to the article, what does the author believe about hot air balloon rides?

    (A) They allow you to fly with birds.

    (B) It's best to go in warm weather.

    (C) It feels like time passes quickly.

    (D) They're convenient transportation.

29. What kind of information will the passengers be given before the balloon takes off?

    (A) The things they are about to see.

    (B) The science behind hot air balloons.

    (C) Tips on how to board the balloon.

    (D) Tips on taking beautiful photos.

30. Where is this article most likely to appear?

    (A) On the website of a travel agency.

    (B) On a sign in front of a historical site.

    (C) In a story about a pilot school.

    (D) In a magazine for photographers.

GEPT
初級模擬試題
第 9 回

09-000

第 9 回聽力測驗

聽力測驗

本測驗分四個部分，全部都是單選題，共30題，作答時間約20分鐘。作答說明為中文，印在試題冊上並經由放音機播出。

第一部分　看圖辨義　◀》09-001～09-006

共5題，每題請聽放音機播出題目和三個英語句子後，選出與所看到的圖畫最相符的答案。每題只播出一遍。

示範例題

你會看到

你會聽到

Look at the picture. What is the man's job?
(A) He is a painter.
(B) He is a reporter.
(C) He is a salesman

正確答案為 (C)。

聽力測驗第一部分試題從本頁開始。

Question 1

Question 2

Question 3

開始時間	
結束時間	

Question 4

Question 5

共10題，每題請聽放音機播出題目和三個英語句子後，再從試題冊上三個回答中，選出一個最適合的答案。每題只播出一遍。

示範例題

你會聽到

Does anyone know how the machine works?

你會看到

(A) Why don't you read this note?

(B) I don't know how to cook it, either.

(C) No one has to work late today.

正確答案為 (A)。

6. (A) I don't work at the gas station anymore.
   (B) There's a train station in the city center.
   (C) There's one two blocks away on the left.

7. (A) I'd like to, but I can't cook.
   (B) Sure. What time should I be there?
   (C) Yes, we hope you can come to dinner.

8. (A) I love playing soccer.
   (B) I enjoy watching golf.
   (C) Playing sports can be fun.

9. (A) OK. When do you need it?
   (B) I'm afraid my cart is broken.
   (C) Sorry, I don't have any money.

10. (A) Yes, I'm going to see the movie on Friday.
    (B) No, I haven't had the chance to see it yet.
    (C) He came out of the movie theater at 8:30.

11. (A) Yes, it's really delicious.
    (B) No, I've never been to France.
    (C) French is my favorite language.

12. (A) I need only one.
    (B) Yes, I like it very much.
    (C) With cream and sugar.

13. (A) I'm a secretary.
    (B) I live in Chicago.
    (C) It's in my living room.

14. (A) I can speak five languages.
    (B) I've only taken an airplane once.
    (C) Yes, I've been to several countries.

15. (A) She's listening to music.
    (B) She'll be back tomorrow.
    (C) She's picking your sister up.

第三部分　簡短對話　◀》 09-018～09-028

共10題，每題請聽放音機播出一段對話和一個相關的問題後，再從試題冊上三個選項中，選出一個最適合的答案。每段對話和問題播出一遍。

示範例題

你會聽到

（男）I can't go any faster.

（女）But the next one is at 1:40. We will be late for the test for sure.

（男）Which platform should we go to?

（女）Platform 2. It's just right near the entrance.

（男）I think we can make it in time.

Question: Where are the man and the woman?

你會看到

(A) At the airport.

(B) At the train station.

(C) In the swimming pool.

___

正確答案為 (B)。

16. (A) Going traveling.
    (B) Trying some food.
    (C) Planning a project.

17. (A) Do some of her work.
    (B) Give her a break later.
    (C) Take a day off with her.

18. (A) He's learning a language.
    (B) He's giving her some advice.
    (C) He's taking an online course.

19. (A) Cancel it completely.
    (B) Hold it next week instead.
    (C) Hold it without the woman.

20. (A) Something less formal.
    (B) The new dress she bought.
    (C) The dress she wore last time.

21. (A) A math problem.
    (B) An English story.
    (C) A history question.

22. (A) Go to a job interview.
    (B) Put money in the bank.
    (C) Attend a work meeting.

23. (A) She may not find her phone.
    (B) The staff took away her phone.
    (C) She will find her phone for sure.

24. (A) The woman's future studies.
    (B) Their memories from college.
    (C) Science and technology
        problems.

25. (A) She has the flu.
    (B) She has a fever.
    (C) She isn't feeling well.

第四部分　短文聽解　◀》 09-029～09-034

共5題，每題有三個圖片選項。請聽放音機播出的題目，並選一個最適合的圖片。每題播出一遍。

示範例題

你會看到

(A)

Mon	Tue	Wed	Thur.	Fri.	Sat.	Sun.
⛈	🌧	🌧	🌤	🌤	☀	☀

(B)

Mon	Tue	Wed	Thur.	Fri.	Sat.	Sun.
⛈	🌧	🌧	🌤	🌤	🌤	🌤

(C)

Mon	Tue	Wed	Thur.	Fri.	Sat.	Sun.
⛈	🌧	☀	☀	☀	☀	☀

你會聽到

Listen to the weather forecast. What's the weather like next week?

This is Good Day weather forecast. It's been hot these days. Are you worried whether it is going to be this hot next week? Then, there is good news for you. We are going to have rain for three days next week which is going to bring down the temperature a little bit. Thursday and Friday are cloudy. And we can expect clear days on the weekends.

正確答案為 (A)。

Question 26

(A)

(B)

(C)

Question 27

(A)

Cinema Timetable	
MOVIE	**Showing Dates**
Toy Story	June 30th-July 20th
Spider-Man	July 14th-July 20th
The Tiger King	July 28th-August 3rd
Car Racing	June 30th-July 6th
Tomorrow Land	July 7th-July 13th

(B)

(C)

Question 28

(A)

(B)

(C)

Question 29

(A)

(B)

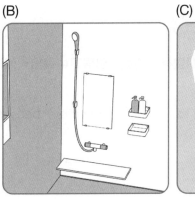

(C)

YEARLY FEES

FIRST MONTH $0
6 MONTH $360
12 MONTH $540

Question 30

(A)

(B)

(C)

本測驗分三部分，全部都是單選題，共30題，作答時間35分鐘。

第一部分　詞彙

共10題，每個題目裡有一個空格。請從四個選項中選出一個最適合題意的字或詞作答。

1. The teacher asked me to _____ my paper because there were some errors in it.
   (A) finish
   (B) revise
   (C) search
   (D) upgrade

2. Please let me know _____ you decide on a date for the meeting.
   (A) while
   (B) once
   (C) until
   (D) though

3. _____ on the birth of your beautiful baby girl!
   (A) Best wishes
   (B) Appreciation
   (C) Compliments
   (D) Congratulations

4. I counted the money, and the _____ amount in the jar was $562.
   (A) total
   (B) least
   (C) equal
   (D) enough

5. You should wear a hat to _____ your face from the sun.
   (A) avoid
   (B) protect
   (C) increase
   (D) improve

開始時間

結束時間

6. We're ready for dessert. May I see the _____ , please?
   (A) price
   (B) check
   (C) menu
   (D) order

7. Pink diamonds are more expensive than white diamonds because they are so
   _____ .
   (A) rare
   (B) useful
   (C) perfect
   (D) ordinary

8. Everyone cheered when our team achieved a narrow _____ at the last second.
   (A) score
   (B) effort
   (C) finish
   (D) victory

9. The toothache was so _____ that I couldn't sleep all night.
   (A) sour
   (B) hurt
   (C) unfair
   (D) painful

10. When Rosalyn tells stories, she uses _____ to make them more interesting.
    (A) languages
    (B) speeches
    (C) practices
    (D) gestures

共8題，包括二個段落，每個段落含四個空格。每格均有四個選項，請依照文意選出最適合的答案。

Questions 11-14

In the past, the train station in my neighborhood was never very busy. But since the new sports stadium opened, it's become ___(11)___ more crowded. Weekends are the worst because that's when they have the big games. I ___(12)___ the sound of the trains, but the laughing, screaming fans always wake me up. ___(13)___ local restaurant and store owners are glad to have more customers, others, including me, aren't happy about the new stadium. I wish I ___(14)___ turn back time and have my quiet and peaceful weekends back.

11. (A) very　　　　　　　　(B) many
　　(C) much　　　　　　　 (D) such

12. (A) use　　　　　　　　 (B) used to
　　(C) am using　　　　　　(D) am used to

13. (A) When　　　　　　　 (B) Because
　　(C) Therefore　　　　　 (D) Although

14. (A) can　　　　　　　　 (B) will
　　(C) could　　　　　　　(D) should

Questions 15-18

Are you thinking about buying a new house? There are many things to ____(15)____ before you begin your hunt. You need to ____(16)____ on the price range, location, house size, and house type. Do you want a home with a big yard for your children to play in? Would you like to live in a convenient neighborhood close to restaurants and a shopping area? It probably won't be possible to get everything on your wish list, so you may have to make some ____(17)____ choices. By thinking carefully about your wants and needs, you should be ____(18)____ to find the right house at the right price.

15. (A) indicate   (B) provide
    (C) receive   (D) consider

16. (A) choose   (B) guess
    (C) decide   (D) figure

17. (A) easy   (B) hard
    (C) likely   (D) strong

18. (A) able   (B) near
    (C) ready   (D) willing

共12題，包括4個題組，每個題組含1至2篇短文，與數個相關的四選一的選擇題。請由試題上的選項中選出最適合的答案。

Questions 19-21

Pacific Ocean Park

We're back with exciting new rides and animal shows!

BUY ONE ticket, GET ONE for FREE!

Bring a friend and share all the fun experiences our park offers.

The Dolphin Aquarium is closed in the evenings

Offer is only for evening hours on weekdays for the next month (17:00-20:00)

Offer is only for students with a student ID

Benson

Hey, did you see the ad for Pacific Ocean Park?

William

Yeah, it sounds like a good deal. We should go this weekend.

Benson

The deal's only good on weekday evenings.

William

Oh, right. That wouldn't give us much time, would it? And after a day of classes, we may be pretty tired.

Benson

True, but we don't have to see everything. And you can't beat the price.

William

OK, you win.

19. Who would be interested in the ad?

    (A) Parents with a kindergarten kid who is crazy about sea animals.

    (B) High school students who want to go to the park in daytime.

    (C) Students who are doing a natural science project on dolphin behavior.

    (D) College students looking for something fun to do on a Wednesday night.

20. What is true about Pacific Ocean Park?

    (A) It's a new park that just opened this year.

    (B) Only students are allowed to visit the park.

    (C) Some changes have been made to the park.

    (D) The park is only open on weekday evenings.

21. What do you think the two people will do?

    (A) Visit the park in the daytime next month.

    (B) Visit the park in the evening this weekend.

    (C) Visit the park in the evening within a month.

    (D) Wait for a better deal before visiting the park.

I love dumplings, a traditional Chinese dish that has been around for over 1,800 years. They can be served as a main dish or snack and come in a variety of delicious flavors and fillings. However, none of those things are why I love dumplings. I love them for the memories they bring back. The best dumplings that I've ever tried are my grandma's recipe. My grandma made special fillings that I haven't been able to find anywhere else. She always made dumplings for Chinese New Year, my birthday, and sometimes other family holidays. When those days come, I miss my grandma even more than usual. My parents and I often make dumplings when we miss her. Even though we can't make dumplings as tasty as hers, it's a great way to keep her memory alive.

22. What is a recipe?
    (A) A way of showing love to family.
    (B) A way to prepare and cook food.
    (C) A way to take care of young children.
    (D) A kind of food that comes from China.

23. Why does the author's family make dumplings?
    (A) To sell dumplings as a business.
    (B) To attempt to create the best recipe.
    (C) To remember a member of the family.
    (D) To enjoy themselves in their free time.

24. Which is likely true about the author's grandmother.
    (A) She is no longer alive.
    (B) She lives in another city.
    (C) She has a good memory.
    (D) She likes to eat dumplings.

Questions 25-27

Dear Mr. Lin,

I'm writing this letter to thank you for everything you've done for our son Derek. I haven't seen Derek this happy in a long time. Before you came, Derek didn't like to go to the PE class because he wasn't as good at sports as other students. On the days with the PE class, he was always worried that he couldn't catch up with his classmates.

However, things have really changed ever since you became his PE teacher. You've taken time to encourage and help him. As a result, he's beginning to improve. Last week, Derek told me that he looks forward to PE class. Even though he still gets nervous sometimes, he's proud of himself for making progress.

Derek has become much more confident thanks to you. Therefore, we'd like to invite you to his birthday party next month. It would be a great surprise for Derek, and we would really like to thank you in person. If you can make it, please let us know!

Sincerely,

Ms. DuPont

25. What is one of the purposes of the letter?
    (A) To thank Mr. Lin for doing so much for Derek.
    (B) To tell Mr. Lin about Derek's learning problems.
    (C) To let Mr. Lin know how much Derek has grown.
    (D) To apologize for Derek not practicing hard enough.

26. Which of the following is true about Mr. Lin?
    (A) Most students get nervous when they are around Mr. Lin.
    (B) Mr. Lin believes that weaker students should work harder.
    (C) Mr. Lin is a kind teacher who is willing to help his students.
    (D) Mr. Lin always asks students to make more effort to improve.

27. Which statement best describes Derek?

    (A) He always feels terrible around his friends.

    (B) He gets upset when he fails to do something.

    (C) He is trying hard and starting to enjoy PE class.

    (D) He used to be one of the top students in his class.

Questions 28-30

Do you often feel sad and lacking in hope for no reason? **Depression**, according to the WHO, is very common, with around 5% of the world's population affected by it. If you or someone you know is experiencing these feelings, it's important to tell to someone you trust. They can offer support and help you find a doctor who can provide you with treatment.

Remember, you are not alone, and there is always help available. There are also things you can do to feel better. Here are some steps you can take:

1. Express your feelings: Sometimes, it helps to express how you feel in a healthy way. You could try talking to a friend or family member, writing in a diary, or even painting.

2. Be more active: Try doing some exercise, even something light. Studies show that exercise can help improve your mood. You can start by walking for just 20 minutes a day.

3. Try a healthy diet: Some people don't feel like eating when they experience depression, and risk becoming loosing too much weight. Others find comfort in food and gain weight. Make sure to eat meals with plenty of meat and vegetables and try to avoid sugar and snacks.

4. Find activities you enjoy: Doing something you like, such as listening to music, reading, or spending time with friends, can help make you happier.

28. According to the article, what is "depression"?

    (A) A WHO program to help people who feel sad.

    (B) A kind of medicine that keeps your mind healthy.

    (C) Someone who can give support to people in need.

    (D) A state of mind where people often feel unhappy.

29. What are the steps in the article for?

    (A) Helping people who feel sad and lack hope.

    (B) Teaching people to be good a friend to others.

    (C) Showing the way to care for family and friends.

    (D) Introducing what courses students can choose.

30. What is NOT something the author suggests to feel better?

    (A) Finding comfort in food.

    (B) Trying painting.

    (C) Getting some light exercise.

    (D) Talking to friends or relatives.

GEPT
初級模擬試題
第10回

10-000

第 10 回聽力測驗

聽力測驗

本測驗分四個部分,全部都是單選題,共30題,作答時間約20分鐘。作答説明為中文,印在試題冊上並經由放音機播出。

第一部分　看圖辨義　🔊 10-001～10-006

共5題,每題請聽放音機播出題目和三個英語句子後,選出與所看到的圖畫最相符的答案。每題只播出一遍。

示範例題

你會看到

你會聽到

Look at the picture. What is the man's job?
(A) He is a painter.
(B) He is a reporter.
(C) He is a salesman

正確答案為 (C)。

聽力測驗

聽力測驗第一部分試題從本頁開始。

Question 1

Question 2

Question 3

開始時間	
結束時間	

Question 4

Question 5

共10題，每題請聽放音機播出題目和三個英語句子後，再從試題冊上三個回答中，選出一個最適合的答案。每題只播出一遍。

示範例題

你會聽到

Does anyone know how the machine works?

你會看到

(A) Why don't you read this note?
(B) I don't know how to cook it, either.
(C) No one has to work late today.

正確答案為 (A)。

6. (A) Yes, it's salty.
   (B) There you go.
   (C) I don't like salt.

7. (A) I'm not sure what time it ends.
   (B) The movie is over two hours long.
   (C) The ticket says it begins at 7:30 pm.

8. (A) I forgot to take it off.
   (B) I bought it at the mall.
   (C) It's really warm in here.

9. (A) Busy! I've been studying for a test.
   (B) I will visit my friends in Hong Kong.
   (C) Tired! I went swimming this morning.

10. (A) Let me take a look.
    (B) Sorry, I'm busy right now.
    (C) Did you try turning it on?

11. (A) No, I haven't made any yet.
    (B) Yes, I've visited a few places.
    (C) I'm trying to fix the problem.

12. (A) Of course you can take a rest.
    (B) No, I've never done it before.
    (C) I don't know what they charge.

13. (A) No thanks, I'm too full.
    (B) You can get another one.
    (C) You can eat the rest later.

14. (A) I got it at the new bookstore.
    (B) I can't think of one right now.
    (C) You can learn a lot from this book.

15. (A) I keep my cups in that cupboard.
    (B) Is this the one you're looking for?
    (C) I just brought a new mug last week.

第三部分　簡短對話　◀》10-018～10-028

共10題，每題請聽放音機播出一段對話和一個相關的問題後，再從試題冊上三個選項中，選出一個最適合的答案。每段對話和問題播出一遍。

示範例題

你會聽到

（男）I can't go any faster.

（女）But the next one is at 1:40. We will be late for the test for sure.

（男）Which platform should we go to?

（女）Platform 2. It's just right near the entrance.

（男）I think we can make it in time.

Question: Where are the man and the woman?

你會看到

(A) At the airport.

(B) At the train station.

(C) In the swimming pool.

正確答案為 (B)。

16. (A) The man broke it.

　　(B) It cost a lot of money.

　　(C) It was a gift to the man.

17. (A) Whether they are going to sing or not.

　　(B) Whether they should call Mary for help.

　　(C) Whether they are on time for the event.

18. (A) Start a new hobby.

　　(B) Give her some advice.

　　(C) Teach her how to cook.

19. (A) An airport.

　　(B) A train station

　　(C) A shopping mall

20. (A) Not worry about the trip.

　　(B) Bring everything they need.

　　(C) Plan the trip for next month.

21. (A) The man forgot to complete the report.

　　(B) The women hasn't received the report.

　　(C) The man didn't send the report by email.

22. (A) Pick a restaurant.

　　(B) Organize an event.

　　(C) Go watch a movie.

23. (A) In the fridge.

　　(B) On the table.

　　(C) In the coffee.

24. (A) Lower the volume.

　　(B) Turn up the music.

　　(C) Stop playing the music.

25. (A) At a park.

　　(B) At an office.

　　(C) At a restaurant.

第四部分　短文聽解　🔊 10-029～10-034

共5題，每題有三個圖片選項。請聽放音機播出的題目，並選一個最適合的圖片。每題播出一遍。

示範例題

你會看到

(A)

Mon	Tue	Wed	Thur.	Fri.	Sat.	Sun.
⛈	🌧	🌧	🌤	🌤	☀	☀

(B)

Mon	Tue	Wed	Thur.	Fri.	Sat.	Sun.
⛈	🌧	🌧	🌤	🌤	🌤	🌤

(C)

Mon	Tue	Wed	Thur.	Fri.	Sat.	Sun.
⛈	🌧	☀	☀	☀	☀	☀

你會聽到

Listen to the weather forecast. What's the weather like next week?

This is Good Day weather forecast. It's been hot these days. Are you worried whether it is going to be this hot next week? Then, there is good news for you. We are going to have rain for three days next week which is going to bring down the temperature a little bit. Thursday and Friday are cloudy. And we can expect clear days on the weekends.

正確答案為 (A)。

Question 26

(A)

(B)

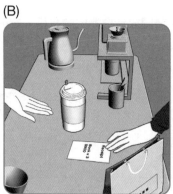

(C)

Question 27

(A)

(B)

(C)

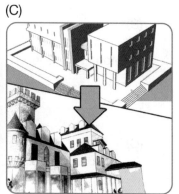

Question 28

(A)

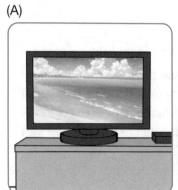

(B)

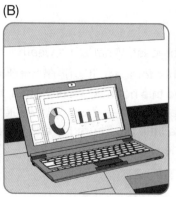

(C)

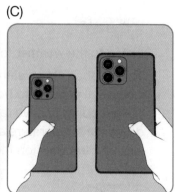

Question 29

(A)

Friday

● ● ● ● ●

6pm - 7pm

(B)

Saturday

● ● ● ● ●

7pm - 9:30pm

(C)

Sunday

● ● ● ● ●

7pm - 8pm

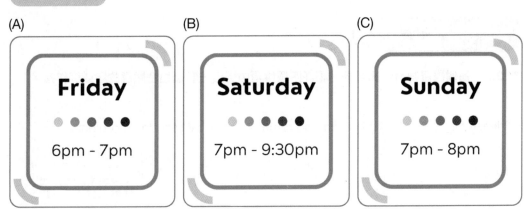

Question 30

(A)

(B)

(C)

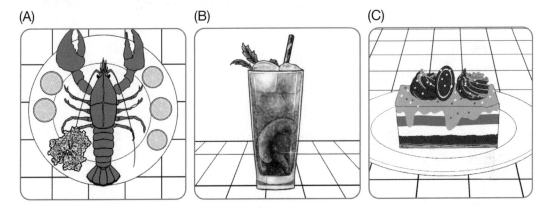

本測驗分三部分,全部都是單選題,共30題,作答時間35分鐘。

第一部分 詞彙

共10題,每個題目裡有一個空格。請從四個選項中選出一個最適合題意的字或詞作答。

1. Please fill _____ this form and return it to me by Monday morning.
   (A) out
   (B) up
   (C) over
   (D) on

2. Can you _____ the kids off at school on your way to work?
   (A) take
   (B) drive
   (C) drop
   (D) send

3. I'm afraid I can't _____ the meeting on Monday.
   (A) attend
   (B) support
   (C) carry
   (D) happen

4. Air tickets to Europe can cost as _____ as a thousand dollars.
   (A) many
   (B) much
   (C) high
   (D) great

5. All groups must have their projects _____ by the end of the week.
   (A) established
   (B) developed
   (C) completed
   (D) indicated

6. After studying cooking, Vivian got a job at a restaurant and started her
_____ as a chef.

   (A) activity

   (B) target

   (C) hire

   (D) career

7. To see the run rise, we have to get up before _____ .

   (A) dark

   (B) scene

   (C) break

   (D) dawn

8. When can we expect to _____ a reply from Ms. Wilson?

   (A) accept

   (B) send

   (C) receive

   (D) gather

9. What you need is a _____ . A lot of people have had their bikes stolen lately.

   (A) police

   (B) lock

   (C) host

   (D) report

10. Good table _____ are a way of showing respect for others at the table.

   (A) manners

   (B) fashions

   (C) scores

   (D) methods

共8題，包括二個段落，每個段落含四個空格。每格均有四個選項，請依照文意選出最適合的答案。

Questions 11-14

Jenny woke up at seven, got dressed, and went to the office, arriving just before eight. She started her day by drinking coffee when she ____(11)____ her e-mail. Next, Jenny went to a department meeting to discuss future projects. Around noon, Jenny took a quick ____(12)____ to eat a sandwich. In the afternoon, she finished a report that her manager needed ____(13)____ the end of the day. At seven, she ____(14)____ her desk before leaving the office after a long, tiring day.

11. (A) checked   (B) watched
   (C) examined   (D) confirmed

12. (A) meal   (B) period
   (C) break   (D) pause

13. (A) on   (B) by
   (C) in   (D) to

14. (A) investigated   (B) organized
   (C) cooperated   (D) exercised

Questions 15-18

What are the most popular pets today? ___(15)___ people love to have dogs as pets. Dogs are known for being loyal and friendly. They need ___(16)___ walks and enjoy playing with their owners. Cats are also popular pets; they are often more quiet and like to explore on their own. Both dogs and cats need lots of exercise to ___(17)___ healthy. It is important to take them to the doctor for check-ups and shots. Having a pet can bring a lot of joy and happiness to a home. Pets can also teach us about responsibility and ___(18)___ others.

15. (A) Many   (B) Any
    (C) Much   (D) Every

16. (A) often   (B) regular
    (C) normal   (D) usual

17. (A) staying   (B) stays
    (C) to stay   (D) stay

18. (A) caring for   (B) care for
    (C) caring to   (D) care on

共12題，包括4個題組，每個題組含1至2篇短文，與數個相關的四選一的選擇題。請由試題上的選項中選出最適合的答案。

Questions 19-21

To	Olivia Miller
From	Pittsburg Art Museum
Subject	Congratulations! You're a winner!

Dear Olivia,

We are happy to inform you that you are a winner at the 19th Pittsburg Junior Art **Competition**. As winner of the Oil Painting Award, your prize will be a full scholarship for four years at the Pittsburg Art School. This opportunity will provide you with training that will set you on the path towards a successful career in the arts.

We would also like to invite you to attend Awards Night, which will be held on September 30 at City Arena. Please dress formally for the evening. If, for any reason, you are unable to attend Awards Night, please kindly inform us by September 18.

Once again, congratulations on the great work!

If you have any questions or need further information, please call the Pittsburg Junior Art Competition Office. We look forward to celebrating your success and welcoming you to Awards Night.

Pittsburg Junior Art Competition Office
Jennifer Rowling

Send

19. What does the word "competition" in the first paragraph mean?
    (A) fight
    (B) quiz
    (C) contest
    (D) meeting

20. Based on the content, how will Olivia Miller probably feel when receiving the e-mail?
    (A) upset
    (B) excited
    (C) impressed
    (D) satisfied

21. What can Oliva Miller expect in the near future?
    (A) To be invited to organize an award party.
    (B) To begin study at the Pittsburg Art School.
    (C) To receive an invitation to attend Awards Night.
    (D) To accept a job offer at the Pittsburg Art School.

Studying at coffee shops is becoming more and more popular among high school students these days. They enjoy studying at coffee shops for many different reasons, including their comfortable seats and convenient locations. They also provide a nice change of environment from home or the library. Another reason is the food and drinks. Students can drink coffee to keep from getting sleepy, and also enjoy a variety of snacks.

However, there are also many students who don't like studying at coffee shops. Loud conversations and music can make it hard to focus. And unlike libraries, there are no available textbooks. Also, the drinks and snacks aren't free like at home. Whether students decide to study at coffee shops or not depends on what kind of environment helps them study best.

22. According to the article, why do some students like to study at coffee shops?
    (A) Coffee shops have an environment similar to that of a library.
    (B) Coffee shops provide a great opportunity to meet new people.
    (C) Coffee shops provide better snacks than what's available at home.
    (D) Studying there makes a nice change from where they usually study.

23. What is the main idea of the article?
    (A) Snacks at home may be free, but snacks at coffee shops aren't.
    (B) There are reasons to study at coffee shops and reasons not to.
    (C) Libraries are better places to study because they are quiet.
    (D) Students like studying at coffee shops because they are convenient.

24. What is NOT mentioned as a reason students don't like studying at coffee shops?
    (A) No available textbooks
    (B) A lack of comfortable seats
    (C) The cost of food and drinks
    (D) Loud music and conversations

Questions 25-27

Hearing loss is common in older adults, and it's important to understand the signs. These include trouble with conversations, trouble hearing certain sounds, and asking for repeats often. When older adults have trouble understanding conversations, like missing parts in noisy places, it is often an early sign of hearing loss. Another sign is finding it hard to hear specific sounds, such as the sound of a doorbell ringing. If someone often asks other people to repeat themselves, like saying "What?" a lot, it could mean they are facing hearing difficulties.

Have you seen any of these signs in an older relative? One possible solution is getting them to use hearing aids—small tools that make sounds louder. Other things that help are facing people directly when talking and finding quiet spots. These steps can make a big difference in improving the daily lives of seniors who are experiencing hearing loss.

25. According to the article, which is NOT a sign of hearing loss?
    (A) When people can't hear the phone ringing
    (B) When people keep hearing sounds in their ears
    (C) When people can't hear parts of conversations
    (D) When people ask others to say something again

26. What is a suggested way to talk to an older adult with hearing loss?
    (A) Stand very close to that person
    (B) Talk to them in a crowded place
    (C) Look at the person you're talking to
    (D) Turn your back while speaking to them

27. What would be the best title for this article?
    (A) *Difficulty Hearing in Older People*
    (B) *Hearing Loss—Signs and Solutions*
    (C) *Ways to Prevent Hearing Problems*
    (D) *The Many Causes of Hearing Loss*

NOTICE
Friday, April 5th

Dear Students,

We would like to inform you that all the computer classrooms in this building will be closed for a week, from April 8th to April 14th. For months, teachers and students have complained about the classrooms being too warm. We have recently found some problems with the air conditioning system. For the sake of a better and more comfortable learning environment during the coming summer, we will have the system checked and repaired during the above dates.

All courses taking place in the computer classrooms will be canceled during those dates. If you need to use a computer while the classrooms are closed, you can talk to your teacher and ask for permission to use the teacher's computer room on the second floor of the office building.

General Affairs Office

Rowland High School

---

28. What is the main purpose of this notice?

    (A) To describe issues with the office building

    (B) To provide an update on new summer courses

    (C) To announce a school event happening in April

    (D) To explain why computer classrooms are closing

29. What should students do if they need a computer next week?

    (A) Wait until after April 14th

    (B) Go to the General Affairs Office

    (C) Use their own personal laptops

    (D) Ask to use the teacher's computer room

30. During what season was the notice most likely written?

    (A) Spring

    (B) Summer

    (C) Fall

    (D) Winter

EZ TALK

GEPT 新制全民英檢初級初試模擬試題 10 回滿分
試題＋詳解

統　　　籌：EZ TALK 編輯部
企　　　劃：潘亭軒
審　　　訂：Judd Piggott
撰　　　稿：歐怡君
翻　　　譯：郭芳吟、田培蓮
解　　　說：郭芳吟、田培蓮
內 頁 插 畫：盛同憶
封 面 設 計：兒日設計
版 型 設 計：洪伊珊
內 頁 排 版：洪伊珊
錄 音 後 製：采漾錄音製作有限公司
錄 音 員：Jacob Roth、Leah Zimmermann
圖 片 出 處：shutterstock.com
行 銷 企 劃：張爾芸

發 行 人：洪祺祥
副 總 經 理：洪偉傑
副 總 編 輯：曹仲堯
法 律 顧 問：建大法律事務所
財 務 顧 問：高威會計事務所

出　　　版：日月文化出版股份有限公司
製　　　作：EZ 叢書館
地　　　址：臺北市信義路三段 151 號 8 樓
電　　　話：(02) 2708-5509
傳　　　真：(02) 2708-6157
客 服 信 箱：service@heliopolis.com.tw
網　　　址：http://www.heliopolis.com.tw/
郵 撥 帳 號：19716071 日月文化出版股份有限公司
總 經 銷：聯合發行股份有限公司
電　　　話：(02) 2917-8022
傳　　　真：(02) 2915-7212
印　　　刷：中原造像股份有限公司
初　　　版：2024 年 11 月
定　　　價：420 元
I S B N：978-626-7516-49-2

GEPT 新制全民英檢初級初試模擬試題 10 回滿
分試題＋詳解 /EZ TALK 編輯部著 . -- 初版 . --
臺北市：日月文化出版股份有限公司 , 2024.11
　面；　公分 . -- (EZ talk)
ISBN 978-626-7516-49-2(平裝)

1.CST: 英語 2.CST: 讀本

805.1892　　　　　　　　　113014180